JAY TINSIANO

Blood Tide

A Doug Brown Terrorism Thriller

DARK **PARADIGM**

Newsletter

To join the Jay Tinsiano reading group head to:
www.jaytinsiano.com/newsletter

- Free books and stories
- Previews and sneak peeks
- Exclusive material

1

It was like the sound of the wind along the coast as the man breathed through the hands covering his face. The darkness was comforting, as was the heat of breath against his palms and fingers. There was regularity. There was order. There was control.

The feeling made sense to him.

His breaths were long and meditative, slowly pulling him away from a world of disappointment and pain. Away from a place where lives are ranked and ordered, giving value to some and making the rest expendable. Away from a planet where the primary species would rather bomb its fellow creatures than admit fault or humble itself to compromise. Away from orders and laughing and crying and pain.

Away from feeling.

The man sucked air through the thin gap between his hands and held on to it. He felt like a bubble, floating up above the world and all of its downfalls, but as he exhaled it all came back.

He had been a soldier once, no more than a boy and stationed far from home. He stood tall, proud and brave, just like the rest of them. The world was a gaping monster that he and his fellow soldiers were ready to slay.

His sergeant called him Blythe, but everyone else called him Ricky. The young man was not large, or very remarkable. In fact, he was the kind of person people walked right by without ever taking notice of. He was invisible most of the time, which is why the officers in the camp took an interest in the first place. Called into the command centre, he was ordered to be ready to ship out the next morning. Blythe was headed to specialist training.

"You will learn a little of everything, Blythe," the captain had informed him. "You'll be the single most sneaky bastard the queen could have prayed for, and we will ensure that you get only the cutting edge information. When we're done with you, Blythe, you'll be a one-man terror cell."

Oh, how right they were.

Blythe took to the training easily, allowed to work at his own pace and not have to wait for the slower wits to catch up. He was trained to use a wide array of weapons, munitions, camouflage, and negotiations. He learned to move undetected – a talent he had already perfected – and to infiltrate even the most heavily guarded facilities. He was encouraged to pursue every avenue, but the one that drew his attention most was explosives.

Blythe loved the way the entire world could be shaken with the single push of a button. Nothing caused such a sudden reaction as a bomb. Drop it from a plane or hide it in a shed; strap it to a building or stuff it in an engine compartment... No matter how they were delivered, explosives were a game-changer.

And that was exactly what Her Majesty's Service was looking to get.

His commanders wanted a soldier who could spread fear and terror all over the globe. They wanted a machine that could penetrate any border and tip an entire nation on its edge. The goal was a delivering device that was fast, intelligent, adaptive, and deadly. What they came up with was Richard Blythe. He was everything and more.

Then came covert operations in Oman.

Blythe was sent to cut his teeth on the Arabian Peninsula in a war Britain officially had no part in, except to advise the Omani troops. Unofficially, they were the backbone of the defence against a well-trained and Chinese armed communist guerilla force.

The fighting was light in his regiment, with very little hostile action breaking out. Blythe was allowed many freedoms though, being encouraged to sneak from one city to another, finding holes in defences and assessing the strength of the enemy. On several occasions Blythe was missing for days without a trace, only to show up hundreds of kilometres away reporting on new enemy movements. Each day brought new successes, but Blythe soon grew bored. He wanted something more.

What he found was Faridah.

The girl was a desert flower who was trapped, concealed and controlled by deeply religious parents. Blythe first spotted her as he was making his way through Al Hajar on his way back to his regiment. She was hidden behind the wall surrounding her father's home, veil and guard both down. Faridah laughed and played with her sisters, freely enjoying the sun and the heat and the company. Blythe was mesmerized by her exotic look, her free and excitable nature, and the bells that sounded in his head every time he heard her voice. She was more alive than any English girl he had met, and he wanted nothing more than to know her.

Days went by, and Blythe kept returning to the girl's home. One evening, Faridah spied him hiding along the top of the wall. She ordered him down as though she was the sultan's daughter, and he humbly agreed.

"Are you American?" she asked with a heavy accent.

"No, miss," he answered softly. "I'm English."

"You look like an American, sneaking around like that," she accused. "If my father found you, he would have you beheaded."

"I believe it," he agreed quietly, staying to the edges of the courtyard. Blythe moved stealthily between the palms and low plants, always maintaining a distance.

"What's your name?" she asked.

"Richard," he answered. "What's yours?"

"Faridah," she sang, and Blythe was lost forever. He spent the next half hour chatting with the girl before slipping back up the wall.

"Can I see you again?" he asked before dropping to the other side.

"That depends on what you want with me," she answered practically. "My parents tell me all a soldier wants is one thing."

"I am not that kind of soldier," Blythe assured her. "I want to be your friend. That is all."

"Then I shall see you again very soon, my friend," Faridah answered.

His heart was alive. Blythe went about his task, scouring the desert and guiding forces against the rebels and troublemakers, but lived only to see her again. The sun beat over the sand and the wind whipped his face, but Blythe took it all in his stride. He was a soldier, but around Faridah he now felt like a man. Their secret romance grew, and soon they began to trust each other more and more. The couple began meeting outside of Faridah's home, instead choosing obscure alleys and abandoned districts. It was in such a place, on a blisteringly hot summer's day, that Blythe and Faridah decided to meet for lunch. Blythe cut through the town like a spectre, weaving between homes and sliding under every eye, until he found the spot described by Faridah. As he approached, though, the sound of a woman screaming could be heard loud and clear, reverberating off of the nearby buildings. Blythe quickened his step when the screaming suddenly stopped

and then discovered his worst fear.

Faridah's body lay limp in the street. Her clothes were torn and her veil had been stripped away. Standing over her was a group of British soldiers, and two of them were pulling their trousers back on.

Blythe was broken. He raced to the command centre to report the crime.

"I'm afraid you may have seen the situation incorrectly, soldier," the lieutenant informed him. "There were none of our men in that region today, with the exception of yourself. It couldn't have happened as you described it."

"But I saw them with my own eyes!" Blythe insisted. "They had raped and killed her!"

"No, Blythe," the officer insisted, frustrated that Blythe wasn't taking the hint. "You didn't see that and, even if you did, what would it matter? This godforsaken country is filled with savages and animals. Sand rats and barbarians, the lot of them. One less girl means at least one less fighter in the future. Whoever they were, I do believe you owe them a bit of thanks for saving you the trouble later on. Now," the commander insisted, "why don't we forget about this whole nasty affair, hmm? I think there is more to do than molly over some girl."

Blythe went on, but he never forgot her. She was his reminder that the world was decorated with an invisible line, and it ran right past all of us. It was the line that separated the rich from the poor, the educated from the ignorant, and the fed from the hungry. It separated you because of how you dressed, or talked, or even by your sex. The line divided people based on religion, nationality, and age. The line was everywhere, in every country and on every inch of land. The line could not be ignored, but maybe it could be broken.

Blythe pulled his hands away from his face and stared into the dim room. He couldn't redraw the lines of humanity, he decided, but he could remove them. Blythe looked over the clippings of his bombings around the world and only saw one thing: Equality. No elites. No paupers. The dust settled on everyone equally, and Blythe loved it. There was a way to make everyone equally weak. It worked in London the first time, and now it was underway in Hong Kong.

"With any luck, we'll tear them all down, right, detective?" he said quietly, only to himself.

2

Most often, it's the screaming that wakes him. It's the cursing and the pleas for help. The cries for someone to make the pain stop and the urge to save just one, any one of the victims. The fire rages in the shape of a bus as the screams roar and the world becomes grey.

Then she appears.

It's a child–a little girl–standing in the middle of the street. She's wearing a plain dress, a wide brim hat, and a doll hangs from one hand. The child stares at him wordlessly as he struggles to get to his feet. The screams in the background begin to fade and he knows that if he doesn't reach them now they will all die, every last one of them. Every inch he crawls cripples the man further. Tears distort his vision and the pain makes him dizzy. He looks up to find the girl standing before him.

"No," he moans, but the girl does not hear him.

It starts as little more than a speck upon her forehead. It's a red dot, pulsing and growing. The dot swells and is dragged from just below the hairline to the brow.

"Oh God," the man sobs. "No, please no."

The red line thickens as it reaches the nose.

"Just let me save them!" the man shouts. "Please! Don't let them die!"

Another speck blossoms beside the first.

"I can do it! I can get them out! There's still time!"

The second speck sends blood streaming down the child's face.

"Get out of my way!" the man orders the little girl. "You get out of my way and let me save those people!"

The bus burns freely behind the girl as blood leaks from her hairline; streaming now as if turned on like a tap.

"No!" the man screams as the bus falls silent. "No!" His declaration fades into a huffing whimper and he beats his fists onto the pavement.

The little girl's face is dark with blood. Red stains the front of her dress in great streaks and splatters as if it was made to be that way.

The man tips his head back and shouts in anguish into the night sky as the doll falls to the ground, followed by the little girl.

"Doug," a woman calls through the descending fog. "Doug!"

Douglas Brown snapped his eyes open and stared into the darkness.

No bus.

No fire.

No child.

No blood.

"Doug?" the woman's voice called again.

He could just make out the silhouette of his wife in the gloom.

"Nightmare?" she asked, knowing full well the answer to that question.

"It's OK, I'm fine, sweetheart," he claimed, rolling away from her. In doing so, he could feel the cold evening air dancing on the sweat from his face, chest, and back. Douglas' hands trembled with the adrenaline rush and it frustrated him that he was doing such a poor job of hiding it from Louise. She had been beside him for so long, and had dealt with so much, he hated making her feel like she had to deal with the nightmares as well.

"It's happening more often," she said into the darkness, concern etched into her tone.

"I said I'm fine," he replied, more harshly than intended. Louise exhaled and shifted her body quickly under the sheet.

"I..." Douglas began, then growled at himself. "I'm sorry," he muttered weakly.

"You should talk to someone," she said for what had to be the thousandth time.

"I will," he lied.

"When?"

Douglas squeezed his eyes closed and fantasised about the night being over. "Soon," he promised.

A hand slipped through the dark and rested on his arm. "I'm worried about you," she said. "I'm worried that you aren't dealing with this. I know you think you are this big, strong policeman who can handle anything, but you can't just bottle it up, Doug. You have to talk to somebody about whatever this is. Is it some old case? It must be something bad, but I know you. I know that you must have done everything you could."

The detective rolled his eyes and wished she would just stop trying.

"The man I know and love would have done anything to help someone in need. I know you gave everything you had for the case, or whatever it was, and I am sure it is not your fault."

Doug pinched his face and strained to keep the sobs at bay. He was determined that he would not cry in front of Louise; not about this or anything else for that matter.

"Doug?" his wife asked in a gentle tone.

"Lou," he began, choking a little on his own voice.

"It's okay," she said eagerly, seizing the moment. "You can tell me," she promised. "I love you and there is nothing you have to go through alone."

"Thanks, Lou, but I just want some sleep," he announced finally.

Louise's hand slid off his arm and disappeared back into the gloom.

Douglas had met his wife while on holiday in Hong Kong. He had been browsing a set of beautifully carved animals on a stall outside a shop in the busy market street. All the animals were from the Chinese zodiac—horses, pigs, tigers, sheep and others. He wondered what sign he was and wandered inside the tiny shop that was filled to the brim with tourist bric-a-brac. A Chinese woman was sitting behind the counter and flashed him the most beautiful warming smile he had seen for a long time. He guessed she was a good fifteen years younger than him but it was hard to tell.

"Hello there. I was looking at the zodiac animals outside and wasn't sure what Chinese sign I am."

Her eyes searched his face. 'Of course. That depends on when you were born.'

"Ah, well, it was a long time ago, that's for sure. It was 1952."

"Ahh, not so old. I am a 1960s woman,' she said. He had guessed right. She looked upwards for a moment. 'And the month?"

"March 2nd," he said, suddenly feeling slightly exposed by revealing his birthday.

She nodded. "That would make you a dragon."

Doug smiled. "That sounds great. I loved the dragon carving. What about you?"

"Oh, I am year of the monkey. Very compatible with dragons," she said, her smile transfixing him once again.

The sounds of the city were faint in this neighbourhood, and the room adopted an eerie stillness. It was so quiet Douglas could hear the seconds ticking by on his wristwatch as it sat on the nightstand.

He knew from experience that getting back to sleep now would be impossible.

Louise bounced awkwardly, flipping her body so that she faced away from him, and exhaled in a blast.

"Lou?" he asked his tone a blend of concern and frustration.

"Goodnight, Doug," the curt reply came.

Douglas huffed quietly and studied the wall on his side of the bed. The images still burned hot in his mind, and he was not ready to relive everything just yet. He slipped his glasses on and took a glance at the clock, which said his alarm would be going off in a couple of hours.

Too short for any real sleep, but too long to just lie here, he decided silently. Doug stayed where he was for a few minutes, watching the moments tick by and listening for his wife's breathing to even out. After he had counted almost twenty minutes, he slowly and carefully eased himself out of the bed.

Pulling out some sweatpants, a pair of socks, and some trainers, Doug wondered if there would ever come a time when he had to tell Louise everything. He held his breath and prayed that he wouldn't. If he would have looked back when he left the room, he may have seen a shimmer welling in the corner of her eye.

Douglas made it to the kitchen and pulled his clothes on. He set a pot of coffee to start brewing and grabbed a bottle of water from the fridge. Young men go for a run in these situations, and old men sit and eat a grapefruit. While Douglas knew he was no longer a young man, he wasn't ready to start acting like an old one either, so he had decided to go for a walk. Coffee would be ready when he got back, and maybe Louise would be up. As he pulled the front door closed he paused, believing that he had heard someone sobbing, but then decided that he was only hearing things.

The crisp morning air felt good on his clammy skin. It would not last, that he knew, and the temperature would rise quickly. A gentle breeze tussled with his grey hair and he adjusted the black frames perched on his nose. The chance to stretch his legs felt good. He sipped his water and tried to focus on nothing except his walk.

He had been back in Hong Kong for a couple of years now, and he loved the city. Not only was it Louise's home, but with the passing of every year, it felt more and more like his own as well. The people were kind, serious but friendly enough. When he put in the transfer request to be moved from the London Met to the Royal Hong Kong Police Force, he had told everyone that it was because he wanted to experience more of his wife's culture. While that wasn't entirely false, that certainly wasn't the only reason for requesting the transfer.

In 1982, Douglas was part of a team that was investigating a serial terrorist. The man's name was Richard Blythe, and he was the most feared person in the UK. During his six week spree, Blythe kept the whole of the nation under arrest. No one travelled without speaking his name. Every man gave his wife an extra kiss goodbye when he left for work and held his children just a little bit longer than usual. The Met was furious, and all efforts were directed towards finding the madman who was responsible. In the end, it was Douglas who located him and brought him in. He was declared a hero, not only in London but all across Europe and even America. He was presented with awards and recognition, and told how much he deserved all of it. They told him he had saved London, but Douglas knew the truth.

Everything had seemed so easy. For a man who had evaded the police for as long as he had, to be caught on the forty-fourth day in such a careless manner, well, the entire experience left a sour taste in Douglas' mouth to say the least. In reality, it seemed more like Blythe was giving up than being caught in Douglas' opinion.

That is until he found out that Blythe was using himself as bait.

It was one of the last great acts of defiance from Richard Blythe, and it left its mark on the soul of the detective inspector. It was a mark that would burn for years to come, never really healing but never getting worse. It was a living, smouldering scar and Douglas knew he would never be rid of it. Streets and buildings would trigger a flashback; the sound of a child's voice; the look in a mother's eye; the honking of a horn; a fire—that one would always produce a reaction in Douglas. Sometimes the attack would be so violent he would have to excuse himself and have a fit in a hallway or a washroom. His body would shudder and his breathing would come in vicious sucks and blasts. Tears would gather between his shoes and the man would hug his stomach and strain to control the rush of panic.

They all died. And he couldn't do anything about it. In forty-four days, Douglas and his fellow teammates had not prevented a single murder, and while the news departments and award-givers promised that Douglas had saved countless lives by catching the terrorist, he couldn't help but feel that Blythe was responsible for that as well.

Blythe had been in control the entire time.

He had claimed he was in a fragile mental state at the time. As a young man, he had served the Armed Forces of the Crown with pride, under the flag of the British Army. He had behaved with honour while serving a tour in Oman in the early seventies but had fallen off the radar after his discharge. According to Blythe's barrister, his mental health had collapsed and he was unable to control his actions. Subsequently, he was convicted on a lesser charge and sentenced to only ten years in prison.

At the time Douglas could not believe it.

He had seen Blythe in action. He had studied this man and his behaviour for weeks and nothing about his process told Douglas of an unbalanced mental state. In his mind, Blythe was just getting away with another type of murder.

Douglas had to be rid of the whole ordeal.

When Louise suggested that she was missing her home, he put in for a transfer that same day, convincing himself that if he changed his location then he might change the effects of the experience as well. His hopes were acknowledged but short-lived, though. As the ten-year mark approached, the nightmares began.

Douglas' feet brought him back to the front step of his modest home. He pushed the key into the lock, but before opening the door he took a moment. There was so much he wanted to say to Louise. There was so much that she deserved to hear. He rested his head against the door and sighed.

'Later,' he decided and pushed the door open. For now, he had to get dressed. There was work to do.

3

"Detective Inspector," the voice called out.

Douglas kept walking, sipping his coffee and snapping a folded newspaper against his leg. The department was so full of detectives, patrolmen, and office personnel, he didn't think twice about ignoring the call.

In London, the desks would be alive with muted chatter and gossip, a low hum filling the space thoroughly. In Hong Kong, the department was a place of quiet organisation, with each agent working stoically upon their own task and very little conversation expected or allowed outside of official business. You answered when you were spoken to and you stuck to the assignment you were given. For many in his old department, this would have seemed more like a work camp than a new and exciting career opportunity. For Douglas, this was exactly the sort of environment he needed after the Blythe case.

Especially now.

"Detective Inspector Brown!" the person persisted in a firmer voice this time, determination characterising his tone.

Douglas stopped, took a long sip of his coffee and turned to face his visitor. "Yes? How can I help?" he answered, still swatting the paper against his leg.

A young Chinese man stumbled over to him, a disorganised pile of papers pressed to his chest in a sprawling mess. "Detective

Inspector Brown?" the man verified.

"Yep," he confirmed, "but please just call me Doug."

"Yes, Detective Inspector," the man replied, dropping a few papers and scrambling to scoop them up.

"How can I help you, Mr...?"

"Ma," the man answered, "Jin Ma."

"Mr. Ma," Douglas said with a tip of his head. "How can I help?" He took a pull from his coffee cup and waited for the story.

"I am here about a Mr. Blythe," he said. "Robert Blythe."

An icy hand latched onto the spine of Douglas at the mention of the name. "Richard," was all he could manage.

"Pardon me?" Jin asked.

"Richard," Douglas repeated. "His name is Richard." He lifted the cup to his lips and paused there. "Richard Blythe," he said, as though reciting a curse.

"Mr. Blythe has been released from incarceration," Jin explained. "As the arresting officer, you are entitled to the facts surrounding his release and supervision."

Douglas huffed and took a sip from his mug.

"He was released two weeks ago," Jin continued.

"Two weeks ago?" Douglas felt the tingles of panic dancing up his neck.

"Yes," Jin replied, shifting the papers against his chest.

"Well," Douglas said in a resigned voice, "thanks for the bad news, Mr. Ma." With that, he turned and resumed his walk to his desk.

"Do you not want to know about his supervision?" Jin asked, following closely behind Douglas.

"Is he being supervised?" Douglas asked, before allowing himself to chuckle without humour. "Not that it will help a man like Blythe."

"He is mentally unstable and it is assumed that he will not have the capacity to escape observation," Jin stated, as though reading the information from a report.

Douglas stopped and spun suddenly to look Jin in the eye. Jin almost bumped into the back of the detective inspector and looked up expectantly at the grey-haired Englishman. "Richard Blythe set off seven bombs and killed sixty-two people. One hundred and fourteen others were sent to the hospital with injuries because of him, and some of them will be scarred for life. He evaded capture for forty-four days until he was apprehended."

"By you," Jin reminded the inspector.

"Yeah," Douglas admitted with a sigh. "By me. So you can trust me when I say that a man who could do all of that will be able to slip past a few bobbies who aren't really paying that much attention anyway."

"So…" Jin began, furrowing his brow in confusion. "Do you want the updates when they come in, Detective Inspector?"

"Just tell me when he escapes their supervision, Mr. Ma," he requested. "Thanks."

"You are not like the other men from England, Detective Inspector," Jin observed. "They are not as … um… What is the word? Hard? They are not as hard as you, sir."

"Probably not," he agreed without a smile.

"And you drink coffee," Jin noted. "I thought only Americans drank coffee and all good Englishmen drank tea."

"I thought all Chinese knew karate," Douglas replied.

"How do *you* know if I know karate or not?" he asked.

"Call it a hunch, Mr. Ma," Douglas answered. "Thanks for the information."

He turned and stomped off to his desk, not bothering to acknowledge anyone else along his way. When he arrived, Douglas set his mug on the desktop and fell into the seat with a groan. "Two weeks," he mumbled to himself. "Two weeks. He's gone by now if he wanted to be."

"Mornin', Douglas," said a familiar voice. "Heard the good news?"

Douglas made a small grunt at his partner, Michael Knightly, which was apparently taken as an encouragement.

"Sounds like they have some leads in the Bishopsgate case," Michael announced.

"It's the IRA," Douglas said, distracting himself with a desk file.

"Well, we already bloody well know that now don't we?" Michael replied. "I mean finding the bastards who did it and bringing them before a judge in the Crown Court." He snorted at his friend's obvious lack of interest. "A man died, Douglas," he reminded him. "Not to mention that they did over three hundred mill in damage and injured forty people. I'd think you'd be excited about finding the ones who did it and holdin' their bollocks to the fire."

Douglas kept searching through the file. "Yeah?" he asked. "And why is that?"

"Well," Michael blurted. "Because of... You know. Blythe and all. He's getting' out soon, I hear."

"He's out already, Mike," Douglas informed him, still fussing with the drawer. Douglas paused just long enough to rub his head and give Michael a serious look. "They let him go two weeks ago."

"No," Michael replied in a disbelieving tone.

"Yes," Douglas corrected. "I received the announcement just now."

"Well, no wonder you're... Well..." Michael swallowed his comment and searched for a new topic. "How's Louise? Still the best-dressed woman in Hong Kong?"

Douglas banged the drawer closed and rested his elbows on the desk. "Do you have any letterhead?" he asked abruptly.

"No, I... Well, maybe," he decided and sat down at his own desk next to Douglas. "You know," Michael said in a delicate tone, "If you need to talk, or something." He drew a small pile of paper out of his drawer and set it on Douglas' desk.

"Sure," Douglas said quickly. "Yeah. Fine. Thanks for the paper."

"Sure," Michael replied. "Who are you writing to?" he asked.

"The London Met," Douglas answered.

"You know they have that thing called e-mail now," Michael reminded him. "You could just send an email, it being the Lord's Year of nineteen hundred and ninety-three an' all."

"Nope," the older man replied. "Don't trust it."

"Phone call, then?" Michael offered.

Douglas scowled at the younger inspector for a moment. "Don't you have some police work that needs your attention, Inspector Knightly?"

Michael simply sighed and took out a handkerchief to mop his brow. "Aye, I'm sure there is."

"Detective Inspector?" came a female voice.

Michael and Douglas turned to see Mei-Xing, one of the young reception staff standing before them.

"There's a boy in reception asking for you by name," she said.

Brown frowned. "Oh. Any indication of what he wants?"

"I'm afraid not, sir. But he's insistent that he sees you. He says it's urgent."

Douglas nodded. "Excuse me, Mike."

Doug Brown arrived at the reception area and saw a child sitting in one of the chairs, dressed in a bright purple shirt and black shorts. He had a red baseball cap pulled down tightly upon his head and an anxious expression on his face.

"Yes, young man?" he asked the boy.

He looked up at the Detective Inspector and walked over to him. "This is for you," he said, holding out an envelope. The moment Michael accepted it from him, the boy turned and ran out of the double glassed doors, as if he were playing a game.

"Hey, wait!" Doug called, but the child was out the door and into the street without turning back. Douglas hurried to the door and looked out on to the street but the boy had already disappeared into the crowded street of a hundred faces.

Mei-Xing came up behind him.

"Shall we send someone after him?" she asked.

Douglas nodded his head.

"Yes, that is probably a good idea, Mei-Xing. Get an officer," he said, staring at the envelope in his hand.

The girl did as he asked and within ten seconds a young Chinese officer was heading out of the doorway in the direction of the crowd.

Douglas held up the envelope to the light and then flipped it over and read the inscription aloud. "The Honorable Detective Inspector Douglas Brown."

He frowned and started to walk slowly back into the station, turning the letter over in his hands as he walked. He stopped at Michael's desk.

"I won't be needing your letterhead, after all, Michael," Douglas announced.

"No?" he asked, looking at the envelope. "What is that?" he added.

"A letter, delivered by that kid," he said. "The postmark is from London. And it's dated nineteen eighty-four."

Douglas looked around him at the quiet office, thinking. It seemed the only sound was a gentle hum of the myriad of rotating fans on desks.

"Eighty-four was the year Blythe was sentenced!" he said, with sudden realisation.

"Doug?" Michael asked, "What's going on?"

And then a similar look of understanding came over Michael's face. "Is that from…"

"I suppose it is," Douglas replied.

"So the address?" Michael asked.

"Was mine," he confirmed. "And the postmark means it must have been delivered."

Michael looked confused again. "So what are you saying?"

Douglas carefully tore the envelope down one side. "I had a mailbox. This came from inside my house," he said matter-of-factly.

"But how?" Michael wondered aloud.

"You don't know Blythe," Douglas answered. He slowly drew out the parchment and carefully unfolded it.

Michael could tell immediately that something was wrong; terribly wrong. The colour seemed to fade from Douglas' face and his expression slowly melted. "Doug?" he asked, holding his hand out for the paper. "Give me the letter."

Douglas' neck flushed and his head began to feel dizzy. The world seemed to spin slowly and the ringing of the past filled his ears. "Not again," he exhaled. The paper slipped from his hand and fell onto the desktop. His eyes grew wide and his breathing stopped. Michael looked down and read the only two words on the page.

Look outside.

"Doug?" he asked, but the man was visibly shaking and obviously trying to compose himself. "Douglas!" Michael snapped. "Is it Blythe?"

The words seemed to bring him back to the moment. Douglas stared up at Michael with wild eyes, and then pushed himself to his feet. "Get down," he said calmly to the room. His colleagues only stopped what they were doing to look back at him, but no one moved from their places.

"Douglas?" Michael pressed.

Douglas flinched as though a realisation had just hit. He grabbed Michael by the shirt and pulled him to the floor, then stood to the face the room. "Everyone!" he shouted. "Get down! Now!"

4

Douglas crashed to the floor, dragging Michael down on top of him.

"Doug!" Michael cried. "What the hell are you doing?" he complained, but the detective inspector stayed on the ground all the same.

"It's him!" Douglas called across the office. "He's here!"

He covered his ears and pinched his eyes and mouth closed, tucking himself into a ball behind the desk. He held his breath, waiting for the explosion.

Moments passed, and still, he held his position. Michael adjusted himself, but still remained hunkered down behind cover. "Doug?" he asked.

Douglas opened his eyes and looked into the worried expression of his partner.

"Is there supposed to be a bomb?" he asked in a delicate voice.

Douglas growled and looked around the room from his position. Men and women were sitting and standing, scattered around the office, and very few had taken cover.

"There's a bomb outside!" Douglas cried. "Everyone needs to take cover!"

A few employees hid themselves behind a desk or a cabinet, while some slipped to the back of the room, looking for shelter or escape, though many of the staff just stood where they were. "How does he know?" someone asked.

"It looks perfectly normal outside," another piped.

"Get down!" Douglas demanded.

"Doug!" Michael snapped. "What did the letter say?"

"It told me to look outside," Douglas panted in a crazed manner. His eyes darted around, wide and amazed at the number of bodies still milling about the office in a curious fashion. Some of his coworkers were coming out of hiding with embarrassed looks on their faces.

"But that letter is like ten years old," Michael pointed out. "It was written before you were ever here," he continued, sitting on the floor with his back against the desk. "Whoever wrote this did so well before anyone could have known where you would end up. There is no way that someone could have planned what you're suggesting."

"He could," Douglas stated, refusing to leave his position.

"But Doug," Michael said in a patient voice, "there is no bomb."

"There is!" Douglas shouted.

Nervous looks wandered toward the pair and Michael waved off their concerns with a hand. "Then let's get a team to sweep the area, huh?" he suggested.

"We need to clear the street," Douglas insisted. "This guy is a maniac, Mike."

"I know," Michael replied in a consoling voice. "But we have no real reason to believe there even is a bomb out there. I mean," he added with a nervous chuckle, "you're saying that an attack was planned more than ten years ago, factoring in prison time and mobility, utilizing assistants..."

"No," Douglas insisted. "He works alone."

"Then how did he recover the letter from your house? Wasn't he in lockup by then?"

Douglas pressed his lips together to make a hard line. For the first time, he was beginning to see things from Michael's position.

"I can't go ordering an entire neighbourhood to be cleared because you got startled by a letter, right?" Michael asked with an understanding smile. "I'll send a patrolman out to look over the street for anything suspicious, and we'll take the letter over and have it analyzed. Okay?"

Douglas sat up and rubbed his eyes, fighting the fear that he was looking like a fool in front of the entire department.

Michael got to his feet and brushed the seat of his pants. "Let's get—"

The first thing they felt was the shockwave, blasting the desk and debris into their bodies. The sound of the explosion rocked Douglas' ears, driving wedges into his temples and making his eyes burn. Bodies crumbled into contorted shapes, flying inwards towards the inner wall as fragments of glass from the office windows broke apart from a powerful force.

The world then fell silent under the ringing in his head, and Douglas quickly patted himself down, looking for any serious wounds. Satisfied that he was still in one piece, he looked around the room. Somehow he had ended up on his back, scrunched up against another desk, pieces of the glass scattered around him. He rolled over quickly to his hands and knees, and scanned the room, wincing at the scene around him. Men and women contorted their faces in silent screams, holding hands against wounds that pumped blood past shaking fingers. An officer with a burn mark across his face went shuffling by in a hurry, holding an arm to his chest. A woman stood a few meters away, turning a slow circle and staring into dead space while the bloodied tatters of her arm dangled freely, decorating the floor around him with dark red droplets.

The ringing began to fade, and the world around him imploded in sound. Silent faces began to produce screams and sobs, while a car alarm blared somewhere outside. Sounds of the building entrance crumbling and crashing competed with the noises coming from the people scrambling for safety. Douglas' eyes dropped to his partner, perched on his hands and knees. He was huffing jagged breaths, spraying a mist of blood and saliva with every harsh exhale.

"Michael?" Douglas asked.

"I'm fine," he assured Douglas. "I'm fine."

"My God, man," Douglas said in a shudder. "We need to get clear of here."

"I'm fine," Michael repeated. "I'm fine." The man pushed himself up so he was on his knees and stared blankly at Douglas. Pink spittle dripped from his lower lip as he kept repeating, "I'm fine. I'm fine. I'm fine."

"Mike?" Douglas asked, grabbing his partner by the shoulder. "Mike?"

Still, the man continued to babble. Douglas gave him a bit of a shake, and Michael turned away from him, resting a hand on a nearby desk and trying to stand. He turned and Douglas cried out loud. A piece of glass had wedged itself in the middle of Michael's back, just to the right of his spine. It was large, about the size of a dinner plate, and it was sticking out from his shirt, covered in blood.

"Michael!" Douglas cried, trying to steady the man as he fell against the desk.

"I'm fine," he said again, in a tone that was both emphatic and monotonous. Douglas forced himself to his feet, his back and legs punishing him for his efforts. "I need a doctor!" he announced to the room. "A doctor!"

His plea ended almost as soon as it began. Throughout the building, there was not a single person who was without injury. Everyone was either nursing a severe wound or was sprawled on the floor dead. There were bodies torn in two and broken men clambering hysterically for the exit.

Blood was everywhere, sprayed and leaked from bodies scattered throughout the ruin. Red pools gathered in dirt and stone and office equipment.

There was no sense in calling a doctor for Michael when the whole room was suffering. Douglas decided that he would have to help Michael himself.

"I'm going to get you out of here," he promised the man. "Right now, Mike. You and me. We are getting out of this place. Right?" he asked, draping his partner's arm over his shoulder. Douglas grunted as he rose, pulling Michael to his feet. "Come on, Mike!" he cried through gritted teeth.

Douglas then began to shuffle away from the blast site and toward the back of the building. If he could make it to a car, he might be able to get Michael to a hospital in time.

"Come on, Mike!" he grunted again, dragging the man through the debris.

"Detective Inspector!" called a nervous voice. "Detective Inspector!"

Douglas turned and called out to the man jogging towards him. "Jin," he gasped. "Help me with Michael."

Jin stopped short of them and gave Douglas a peculiar expression.

"Jin!" Douglas blared, losing his grip on Michael's arm.

"But Detective Inspector," Jin began, "look at him."

Douglas could feel the heat of anger rising in his stomach. "What?" he growled, bouncing Michael's weight so he was over his back again.

"He's dead," Jin said in a sad but direct way.

Douglas froze for a moment, feeling the way Michael's frame hung off of his shoulder. He slowly turned his head to look at his partner who was looking into the void, mouth hanging open with blood and spittle making a web on his chin and shirt. Douglas fell to his knees and let Michael's weight slip off of him and fall to the floor.

Jin stood there uncomfortably, fidgeting with his hands and breathing through his teeth. He then looked over the room, pausing on the entryway. The majority of the wall was gone; carved out in a great arched portal. Outside was the smouldering husk of a BMW, blasted almost beyond recognition. Behind was the clear damage of the building across the street, windows and doors blasted out, and all around the hustle of people trying to get away from the burning chaos.

Jin turned back to Douglas and gasped. "Detective Inspector?" he asked, kneeling down to grab him by the arms. Douglas' eyes rolled in his head and he fell back, Jin holding tightly and guiding him to the floor.

The next day Douglas was propped up in a hospital bed, his head delicately balanced to one side. The afternoon light demanded entry to the room, sliced by the half-open blinds and spilled over the sheets and blankets. A bandage was strapped on the brow over his right eye and he was covered in small nicks and scratches, the colour of which seemed obscenely red beside the brilliant white of the bedding. His breathing was steady, but his eyes told of a volatile storm raging within his mind.

A knock at the doorframe made him jump and a small squeaking noise escaped his lips. Standing in the doorway was the chief inspector, Christopher Johnson.

"May I come in, Douglas?" he asked in a soft tone.

Douglas chose not to reply, but nodded and rested his head back against the wall of pillows behind him. Johnson accepted the gesture as consent and pulled a chair to the bedside.

"I know you won't be ready to talk about the incident for some time," he began.

Douglas didn't say anything, instead stared at the T.V. screen that silently replayed news footage of the police station bombing. He had long since muted the volume.

"And the panel is debating how long you should be on paid leave," the commander continued, "Now, I'm not going to ask you to participate in anything you aren't prepared to handle."

"Not prepared to handle?" Douglas asked in an offended tone, looking back at Johnson with a frown.

"It's no secret why you left London," he replied. "And there's no shame in it. Soldiers don't go back to the war zone unless they must, and everyone understood why you wanted to leave the scene of so much pain."

"Oh did they?" Douglas asked, clearly irritated by the track the chief was taking. "None of you know this man. Not one of you. They said he was insane, and he is, but it's a calculated insanity. He doesn't see the world like the rest of us, and he will not stop until his goal is accomplished. He's a soldier," Douglas reminded him, "and once he identifies his target he will mercilessly pursue the mission."

"Which is what, exactly?" Johnson responded, leaning forward in his chair.

Douglas stared at the chief, terrified by the words he was about to speak but unable to prevent them. "Last time," he began, "Blythe was attempting to overthrow society itself. His every move was choreographed into a dance that was designed to bring London to its knees, and it worked," Douglas admitted with a dark laugh. "My God man, it worked. In a matter of a few days, Blythe had the city tearing itself apart. Entire businesses shut down indefinitely, pledging to stay closed until the crazed bastard who was responsible was caught and locked behind bars. Schools ran special evacuation drills and Scotland Yard had most of the boys running all day and all night. The streets were filled with patrolmen, yet Blythe still moved wherever he wished, whenever he wished, and he did whatever he wanted."

"Until you caught him," Johnson offered.

"Until he gave himself to me," Douglas corrected. "Blythe didn't get caught, chief. He gave himself up. There's no other way to describe it."

Johnson mused silently, staring at the floor for a moment before asking, "And what do you think he wants this time?"

"More of the same?" Douglas suggested, humming at his own question before answering, "Maybe. But then again, maybe not."

"He sent you this," Johnson announced, drawing the letter from his coat pocket and setting it on the bed. "You're the contact person in all this. Is the department the target?"

"I don't know," he replied honestly. Douglas stared down at the envelope for a time before reaching out and taking it again.

"When you opened it, was it just the letter and the seed?" Johnson asked. "Or was there anything else?"

"Seed?" Douglas answered with a scowl. "What seed?"

"In the envelope," Johnson insisted. "There was a seed. I left it in there."

Douglas pried the envelope open and inspected the contents and removed the letter. Sure enough, there was a seed at the bottom of the envelope. Douglas turned the envelope over and poured the contents into his hand, where he pinched the seed between his forefinger and thumb, holding it up to get a closer look at it.

Suddenly a darkness fell over his expression, causing Johnson to ask if Douglas was still alright.

"Did you ever read Sir Arthur Conan Doyle?" Douglas asked.

"You mean the Sherlock Holmes stories?" Johnson clarified. "Well, yes, as a younger man I did read a few."

"Do you remember 'The five orange pips'? In the story, orange pips sent by mail are referenced as a warning to the recipient that they will die in an unexpected way."

Douglas looked at the Chief. "It's his twisted humorous way of telling me I'm the target."

5

London - 1982

"Don't worry, Brown," Superintendent Sheridan said in a commanding tone. "We'll get this bastard."

Doug ran his hand over his face and sighed in a huff. "Forty-three days, Sherry," he reminded his captain. "Six bombs in less than six weeks."

"I know," he replied, in a voice that still rang with confidence.

"Forty-four people dead and more than one hundred injured," Douglas continued. "And frankly," he added in a low, harsh voice, "we are no closer today than we were when we started. This guy has been ahead of us at every turn. He's playing with us, Super."

"Brown," Sheridan said, holding up a hand, "we will find him, and we will bring him in."

Douglas leaned back in his chair and rested his hands over his eyes. The department around them was buzzing, though it was missing the optimistic tone that had become so commonplace over the past few years. The recession was hitting the area hard enough, with over three million people out of work in Britain, but to have this maniac running all over the city, blowing up shops and cars, put the entire city on its heels.

"He has been playing with us," Douglas repeated in a tired voice. "We have done everything right," he said, sitting up straight and staring at the mess of papers and photos scattered over his desk.

His eyes lifted and he gazed across the floor, past the sea of desks, towards the oblong windows that overlooked Victoria Street. "We have followed every procedure and obeyed every rule, and this guy is still just out there walking around. He is setting off a bomb a week. We have the streets flooded with patrolmen, and men working 'round the clock, and that son of a bitch is just milling about as happy as you please…"

"Brown," the Superintendent interrupted a slight edge to his tone.

"We have done everything just as we were told, and this man is doing whatever he damn well pleases," the inspector insisted. "We must begin the job of redefining our role in this operation if we are going to have any chance of catching this man."

The Superintendent sighed and crossed his arms over his chest. The cold truth was Douglas Brown was right and Sheridan knew it. They had nothing on the bomber. No name. No serious leads. The profilers said he was male and former military, based on his techniques in creating and detonating the hardware. He would have to be at least eighteen but was probably no more than sixty they said, which didn't exactly narrow the search very much. At each of the crime scenes, the inspectors were unable to discover any sign, witness, or clue that would help them to narrow their search. As of that moment, for all intents and purposes, he was still completely anonymous. The Met was pressed hard from all directions to catch this man. The Crown had ordered their best agents to assist in the investigation, and several other world powers had offered the same. The world was watching as London was taken to pieces, one blast at a time. Systems were reinvented to ensure that all procedures were followed, believing that if every *i* was dotted and *t* crossed, then they were sure to find their man, though, at this point, Douglas was beginning to have doubts in the process.

"We stick to the books," the Superintendent reminded him. "We follow the guidelines, and we catch this man through scrupulous police work. We will get him, Brown. Eventually, we will get him."

"After how many more explosions?" Douglas asked in a hopeless tone. "After how many more men, women, and children are lying dead in the street? After how long?"

"He will slip up," Sheridan promised. "They always do."

"I am not prepared to sit about hoping that the single most successful serial bomber in Britain's history makes a mistake!" Douglas blared, rising to his feet. The room fell silent, and all eyes drifted toward the frame of the inspector. "We have nothing on him!" The Superintendent shifted uncomfortably under such a public display of their present failures, but Douglas pressed on. "He is attacking us at will with absolute freedom. For God's sake, man! Everything we say we know about him is an assumption. Race? Sex? Age? Motive? We have nothing, and he is picking this city apart, tearing us to pieces in our very homes. The city is terrified and, honestly, we should be as well. We are in the middle of the largest manhunt I have ever known, with agents and police from half a dozen international agencies all pouring over the information, and not one man or woman has given us anything we can use. The man is a ghost! He goes where he pleases and attacks at his leisure while we scramble behind him, picking up the pieces."

All around the office, officers and inspectors watched with disheartened expressions. Douglas knew that they were giving this attempt their all, but he was also very aware of the fact that it was not getting them any closer to the bomber.

"Douglas," Sheridan began, struggling to maintain his composure, "every investigation has its moments such as these. There are always seasons where the trial seems cold."

"Seasons?" Douglas replied with a cynical laugh. "You are describing our every effort."

"And what do you suggest?" the Superintendent replied, his emotions steadily, slowly boiling over. "Hmm? Do we just hand over the country to this man? This madman? What are you suggesting, Brown? That we just dust our hands and leave him Britain?"

Douglas shook his head at the reply, feeling more frustrated with the state of the police force than ever. "I'm saying that if we try something and it doesn't work, then there is no reason to assume that continuing in that direction will ever produce the desired result. We need to change how we are hunting this man."

Several officers around the department nodded and a few voiced quiet approbations. Sheridan looked about and exhaled in a frustrated snort.

"Super," Douglas said in an unwavering voice, "I think it would be best if you give me a small team to reevaluate the scenario and start looking for this man using alternative means."

"Alternative," the Superintendent replied, "or illegal?"

"I want the freedom to operate beyond the confines of our normal procedures since our current guidelines are proving to be completely ineffective." Douglas let the statement sink in but continued before his commander shut him down. "I feel that it would be the best direction for the investigation and the safety of this city."

"I feel," Sheridan began, "that you would do yourself a favour by stepping away from this investigation for a short break."

"Excuse me?" Douglas asked in disbelief. Officers around the room looked on in silent wonder.

"Just for a few days, at least," he elaborated. "I think the stress of the environment is proving to be a lot for all of us, and I am willing to bet that a short rest from this environment will do you some good."

"Sir," Douglas said in a barely controlled voice. "You need every available mind on this investigation."

"And I am afraid that I do not have yours at this moment," the Superintendent answered. "You are not yourself, Douglas. I need you in top shape."

"The next bomb is imminent," Douglas reminded him.

"And with any luck, this will be the one where we catch him," the Superintendent said, trying to embolden the staff listening in. "But you are a risk to yourself and this agency if you stay. So, Douglas, if you please, do not make this harder for any of us. I am commanding you to take a leave of absence of no shorter than one week."

"One week?" Douglas repeated in a horrified voice.

"To ensure your health and well-being during this investigation," the Superintendent continued, doggedly. "You have worked as hard if not harder than most, and are more deserving of a break than many. So please," he said in a fatherly tone, "do go home and rest, Douglas. I will see you here in seven days."

"Sir, this investigation cannot afford to spare even one able body."

"This investigation cannot afford to have an inspector who has been worked beyond his limits," the Superintendent answered.

"But, sir, if you will just permit me to—"

"—Go home, Douglas," Sheridan said flatly. "That's an order."

The world suddenly grew very silent. Tensions were high in the department, and anxiety was rampant as everyone tried to guess where the next bomb would be reported. No one was comfortable and everyone felt overworked, but Douglas was unable to break off. Not now. He needed to see this through. He needed to be there when it ended. He had invested too much time and effort, and endured sleep deprivation, in searching for a man no one could identify. It wasn't a matter of principal. It wasn't a matter of duty. To Douglas, it was more than that. It felt as though his very sanity depended upon the capture of this man who had plagued his dreams and soiled his days for too long.

"Superintendent," he said quietly.

"No, Douglas."

"Put me on a new team. Put me on patrol. Put me at a desk in the Yard." His voice teemed with the battle that was being waged inside his mind. "Do not send me home," he pleaded, emotion muting the words slightly. "Do not send me home to think and worry and do nothing. It'll make me mad. It will. Please, do not send me home."

"Tell you what," the Superintendent said, forcing a smile that no one believed. "Take a little holiday."

"A holiday?" he replied in disbelief.

"A holiday," Sheridan confirmed. "Go someplace quiet. Compose yourself. Get yourself together and then come back into the fight with a new set of eyes. We'll be here when you return."

"A fucking holiday?!?" he boomed, rattling the ears of everyone in the office.

"Doug," the Superintendent said in a tone of warning.

"So I'm supposed to go fishin' while a madman blows up my home? " he said cynically. "A holiday?" he asked, screwing his face up as though trying to understand what was wrong with his superior.

"You are in no state to perform your duties, Doug," Sheridan informed him in a tone that was straining to be quiet but firm.

"No state," Douglas chuckled in a shocked and hurt voice. "Fine.

Fine. I'll go. But you know what? I can't just sit and wait. I can't just plod around and do nothing."

Sheridan rested a hand on his inspector's shoulder and looked him in the eye. "Try," he encouraged.

As Douglas gathered a few items from his desk, he noticed an envelope with his name handwritten upon the face. He picked it up and flipped it over. It was sealed, with nothing else written beyond 'Douglas Brown'. He looked around, as though someone standing close by might claim it. Everyone seemed to be avoiding eye contact after his outburst with the Superintendent, so Douglas was essentially alone in a room full of people. The inspector tore the envelope open and pulled out a simple card with two words written in the same style in which his name had been written.

Look outside.

6

"Do not be fooled," Douglas told the small group gathered at the makeshift police station. "This man is not through. He will not stop at a single attack. He will most certainly hit another target in a similar manner, and in another part of the city."

A hand rose and Douglas pointed to the officer.

"Will it be another police target?" the man asked.

Douglas looked to Johnson who shook his head.

"It is unclear at this time what his next target may be," Douglas announced to the room. "While on patrol, all of you should be on the lookout for any activity that seems suspicious. Cars parked in areas where it's not typical. Men carrying large duffels for no apparent reason. Persons, especially white men in their forties, who are taking pictures of buildings, monuments, or official offices."

"Detective Inspector," a patrolman called out, raising his hand.

"Yes, Jun?" Douglas answered.

"You have just asked us to stop half of Hong Kong," he pointed out. "Cars parked where they don't belong? Men carrying large bags? White men taking pictures of important sites? We could stop a thousand people a day with those instructions."

"You are to focus your attention and efforts on looking for Blythe specifically," Johnson answered. "Review the photos of him and his previous delivery systems. If you see anything that possibly matches, I want you to stop him for questioning. Male or female. Young or old. If it matches any of the pics, you will interject. As for the rest of it," he added with a sideways look to Douglas, "do your jobs. If people are being suspicious then go check it out. If it looks like something is off, or wrong, then get in there and get to the bottom of it. This maniac will not be satisfied with just one show. He set off seven bombs during his last spree in London. The man is patient, careful, and is highly skilled with explosives. He will not make any of the typical mistakes, so we can't just sit around and wait for him to slip. We're going to need to run him down, and fast."

"The good news is," Douglas added, "the last time he was at it, Blythe set off a bomb about once a week. That means we should have another five or six days to flush him out. And I can't emphasize enough how right Chief Inspector Johnson is about this man. Blythe is a killer, but he isn't out of control. He is methodical and driven. Blythe is not going to just appear on a street corner, and he isn't just going to turn himself in." Douglas paused to push away a memory that was crawling up his spine. "He evaded capture for six weeks because we did things defensively, waiting for him to make the mistake that never came. We will not make that error again."

"You have your orders," Johnson said. "Now get out there and find this maniac."

The room was filled with the sounds of chairs scooting and books closing, but it was the more subtle noise that interested Douglas. It was the murmuring. Out of the corners of their mouths, the officers were muttering to one another, expressing concerns to their fellow patrolmen but not directly to Brown or Johnson.

"Doug?" Johnson asked, seeing his friend and subordinate staring over the staff.

"They know," he answered.

"Who?"

"Everyone here. They know that Blythe is after me," Douglas worried. "They don't know how they know, but they do."

"Nonsense," Johnson assured him. "They're professionals. They know what the job is, and they'll be putting all of their efforts into finding Blythe."

Christopher and Douglas exchanged a glance, though Douglas' unimpressed scowl revealed some unspoken feelings.

"I know," Johnson told him. "I know."

"I don't think you do," Douglas shot back, watching as the room emptied. When the last man was out, he let it rip. "They aren't idiots, Chris. They're coppers. They can already see the connection."

"Don't worry about this," his supervisor suggested. "It's not how you think it will be."

"Oh yeah?" Douglas panted. "What do London and Hong Kong have in common? Bombs and me. Blythe sent me the note. I called for everyone to hit the floor before the bomb hit, proving to everyone that I was directly involved. I'm the focus of this one, and our people get spooked by this, there won't be a single one of them that will want to be within a mile of me at any time. And that's not mentioning what will happen after the third or fourth bomb. They'll be blaming me for all of it. Shit, Chris. Eight people are dead, and more than thirty have been severely injured. The station is a disaster. What happens when a family member dies? What happens when a child gets blown to bits? I'll have a gun to my head in no time."

"Douglas," Johnson sighed, without making an attempt to continue.

"I want this son of a bitch more than anyone else," Douglas

promised, "but this time it has to be different."

"It will be," Johnson said confidently. "This time he won't have free run of the city because every officer and news agency has Blythe's picture. He hit our house, killing our own, so every copper is desperate to run this guy down. We will be on him so fast he won't know what happened."

Douglas hummed and shook his head. "You don't know Blythe."

They stood in the street that had been closed off, looking into the yawning hole that used to be the front of the police station. They spotted the occasional glimpse of forensics shifting through the damaged building behind sheets of plastic that shielded the scene.

"I'm amazed he only killed eight," Johnson remarked.

It was the only thing either one of them had said for a while. The shock they both felt as the men peered into the rubble was stupefying. This wasn't just a hole so big you could park a truck in it, this was more like a great start to an expressway tunnel.

Douglas turned a circle in the street. They were standing at the epicentre of the blast, right where the car had been.

"He must have had this thing loaded to the teeth," Johnson remarked. "A hole that size? God damn. I don't even know how large of a device he would need for that."

Douglas eyed the building across the street, then drew his gaze up and down the avenue.

"The boys are working the numbers though," the chief inspector continued. "They'll have the stats back soon and then we'll know more about what we're dealing with."

"You're thinking about this all wrong," Douglas replied in an absentminded voice. "You can't look back with this guy." He raised his line of sight up the side of the police building then eyed the office complex opposite the police station. "They'll tell us what type of explosive they think he was using and how much they think was in that car, but that's just classic police work. It didn't help last time, and it won't help this time either." Douglas rubbed his neck and looked at the ground around him. "We don't need stats. We need motive, and direction."

"Yeah. The pips," Johnson reminded him. "You said he was gunning for you."

"Then why didn't he kill me?" Douglas asked in a distracted voice.

"Pardon?" Johnson asked, scrutinizing him.

"Look at that," Douglas said, pointing at the face of the station. "Now look over here." He pointed across the street at the office complex. "What do you see?"

"Broken windows," Johnson answered with a shrug. "A little debris."

"It's just a little farther off than the station from where we are, and yet the damage is nowhere near as bad," Douglas explained. "Look up and down the street and it's as though nothing happened at all. Blythe wasn't just targeting the police station, he was leaving the rest of the world out of it. You said it yourself," he added in an excited tone, "most of the deaths were police. He set off a car bomb on a busy street in Hong Kong. How the hell did he do that and not kill a hundred people? Sure, there were thirty-some critical injuries, but the medics estimated the minor ones in the one-twenty to one-thirty range. He scratched the world. He scared them. But let's face it, he was also careful not to hurt them too badly."

"What are you saying, Doug?" Johnson asked through eyes pinched into slits.

"He delivered that bomb at us." The words seemed to float

around them, hanging in the air. "If he has the patience to protect the lives of a hundred people while setting off a car bomb on a busy street and he wanted me dead, then trust me, I'd be dead." Douglas raised his eyes to the rubble. "Do you see Michael's desk?"

The Chief Inspector rubbed his mouth and took a deep breath. He looked into the station and said, "Yes."

"All of the worst damage was done before that point. He knew exactly how far away I would be, and adjusted his device for it."

Johnson did not like where this was going.

"He's not just targeting me," Douglas continued. "He's targeting police."

"That's a lot of prep and precision for only having just been released."

"Two weeks was more than he needed," Douglas said confidently.

"Doug," Johnson sighed. "You mentioned Michael."

Douglas held his eyes on his dead partner's desk, his expression growing slightly darker.

"I haven't seen the release from the psych yet," Johnson announced. "I shouldn't even have you on this. You should be at home, resting."

Douglas harrumphed quietly. "Like some retiree? Like some senior citizen? I don't think so, Chris."

"I'm not saying that you can't help," Johnson began, but Douglas talked over him.

"You aren't sending me to go sit at home and wait for a bomb that's sure to come." Old feelings came welling up. He was reminded of the last time he had this talk, with his previous boss, Sheridan. "No. I'm fit. I'm staying on."

"But this cannot be a vendetta case," Johnson insisted. "I can't afford to have you running into danger with your gun drawn like some foolish cowboy from the States. I need level heads.”

“Then you need me,” Douglas returned. “Did you see the faces around the station? Did you see the looks in the eyes of the officers in the meeting? Did you hear how they spoke? They want this guy dead. They feel personally attacked. They are going to need this to be over fast, and if they even begin to tie me into this, or blame me for the deaths of their friends and colleagues, then the entire department will collapse like this building,” Douglas promised, waving at the wreck before them.

Johnson made a small growl and looked away.

“Here’s what we know,” Douglas said, returning to the topic. “He’s targeting coppers. We need to get the word to the boys because we won’t just stumble across the next explosion. It’ll be a trap.”

The Chief nodded but remained silent.

“We can expect that it will be fatal if it isn’t stopped, but the average bystander will probably be safe.”

“Doug,” Johnson inserted. “I’m still not sure you are completely up to this. I mean... The guy looks like he is blowing up officers just to get at you. How can you stay focused when that’s happening? I’m going to talk to the psych today.”

“I’m fine,” Douglas maintained. He exhaled a long and shuddering breath. “I’m just thankful we have a few days to clean up and try to run him down.”

◇◇◇

Across the city, officers sprawled into every dark corner and down every lane, searching for anyone who fit the description. The police were stopping local Chinese and foreign ex-pats alike, anxious to capture the bomber before another explosion hit. Word had just come over the radio that the suspect may be targeting police sites. Security had been increased across Hong Kong at all of the station locations and government buildings. No cars were allowed to stop in front of any official location, and all persons in the area were being stopped in the street and searched thoroughly if they appeared the least bit suspicious.

Everyone was on edge.

Two officers working downtown cruised slowly up the main drag, eyeing pedestrians and anyone sitting in a parked car. The driver tapped his partner's elbow and pointed down an alley. About seven or eight meters into the shadow, there was a man kneeling over a bag. He was wearing a long dark coat and hat, and he had his back to the street. The driver parked the car and got out, his passenger right at his heels. They called out, but the man just kept working over his bag, right in the middle of the gap. Again the officers cried out to him and again they were ignored.

The first officer drew his sidearm and the nodded for the second to do the same. They slowly approached the man, warning him to stop what he was doing and turn around. As they got closer the first officer let out a sigh. He told his partner that it wasn't a man after all. The bundle was just a coat and hat, which he grabbed up as proof. The second officer yelled and pointed at the bag, but too late. The alley was filled with light. An explosion erupted throughout the confined space, and tiny bits of shrapnel dug into everything around the bag. Holes appeared in the brick of the buildings and the bodies of the officers. The first was shredded by the blast. The partner was partially shielded by the driver, though he took several pieces to the face. He writhed on the ground for a spell, listening to the ringing in his ears and the screaming in the streets, as his life poured out into the drain.

At the opposite end of the alley, a man lit a cigarette and strolled calmly away.

7

"Inspector Brown," the psychologist sighed. He had one leg draped over the other while his finger tapped fitfully at his knee. "I will be unable to give you clearance if you aren't willing to participate fully."

Douglas carefully picked at some dead skin around a thumbnail. "You have my full and complete cooperation, doc," he promised, not taking his eyes off his task. "I am completely fit and ready for service." He had said those words a lot lately, to his fellow inspectors, his commanders, his wife.

"I'm sensing that you are distracted," the doctor explained. "It would seem that you are wrestling silently with something, and if there was ever a time or place to talk about it, then now would be the perfect opportunity."

Douglas pressed a fingernail hard against a small flap of dry skin hanging on at the base of the nail. He dragged his nail, tearing the sick piece away from the healthy. He looked at the curled, ragged bit stuck under his nail for a moment before flicking it to the carpet.

"There was another explosion..." the doctor prompted.

Douglas' eyes cut to the psychologist, his glare saturated with hatred.

"That is the third bombing in as many days," the doctor continued. "This last was an attack upon a police officer's patrol car.

Was he on duty at the time?"

"It hasn't been three days," Douglas corrected, still glowering at his evaluator. "Blythe has attacked once every eighteen hours."

"Exactly?" the doctor asked, his face darkening with curiosity.

"Exactly," Douglas confirmed, "which means we are due for another visit in just under five hours."

"How can you be so sure?"

"It's Blythe, doc," Douglas answered, as though that would explain everything. After a pause, he continued. "The man is detailed, specific, and intentional. He does things on purpose, even sick things. Nothing is by chance. He's a perfectionist. I've met him. I know. That next bomb will go off on time, and the boys have only a few hours to figure out where so they can stop it. All we know is that he will attack a police target, so everyone is on guard and watching out for each other, but Blythe would have planned for a large-scale hunt. He would have considered our reaction and adapted to stay ahead. Every turn with this man is a left one. He doesn't follow the rules and as a result, he doesn't get caught. There's a genius to his madness, though. If we find it, and if we're damn lucky, then we might have him."

"Why eighteen?" the doctor asked. "Why not set off a bomb every twenty-four hours? Or every ten? Eighteen seems like there may be a specific intention there."

"It was the number of people killed in the final explosion before he went to prison," Douglas growled, picking at a new piece of dead skin on his hand. "And if you ask me, every hour that goes by is another reminder that he was only caught because he wanted to be caught."

"You say he's detailed? Careful? That he only works with specific intention? Those types can be a very difficult case, I would imagine. The mind that would be required to perform not only a mass attack on human life but to do it in the manner you are describing, well that would be a fascinating study indeed. You say he wasn't captured last time, but that he set himself up to be caught. Why do you think that is, inspector?"

"If I knew his plan, doctor," Douglas replied with a mild level of scorn, "then I would have him already." He kept his eyes on his hand, digging away at a spot of dried skin.

"If he is as you say, he probably doesn't act in the same manner twice," the doctor supposed. "His execution will have a pattern, but he will take care not to repeat his movements. Each attack will be its own work of art in his mind, and while the brush strokes will be similar, they will all be very different. The attack on the station. The alley bomb. The car bomb. Each of them will look like Blythe, but the execution will be unique."

Douglas laughed and eyed the psychologist through his eyebrows. "That would imply he followed the rules. The car bomb? That wasn't a first for him. Shit. He used the same type of bomb in front of the station. In London, three of the seven bombs were stuffed in cars, and yet we still have no idea how he did it. I mean... How do you get inside the station garage, totally undetected, with a pipe bomb the size of a bread loaf, strap it to a patrol car, and then sneak out without ever being stopped or questioned? He left nothing behind. No signs of entry, or clues of any type. Hell, we don't even know if he placed the bomb at the station. It's just that we can't think of another option for him. You can't exactly crawl under a patrol car while it's parked on the street, can you? And once he had everything set up, how did he set off the bomb? Was it a timer? A remote? The boys are tearing the wreckage apart but they can't seem to find enough to tell them anything. There are parts that could be a receiver, but who knows?

"Another thing. How in the hell did he know where that car

would be headed that day? I mean, there were a dozen units on that side of town, scanning all over. The officers have no routes or patterns. They patrol at random, driving where they feel and answering calls. The officer who was killed was responding to a noise complaint. Blythe got him en route. How would he know what car would respond where, and when it would happen? I don't think it was a timer since Blythe would need more control than that."

"I agree," the doctor added, though Douglas didn't need him to at the moment.

"It had to be a remote of some kind," he continued. "But that would mean he had eyes on the car. How could you plan that, unless..." Douglas' eyes glazed over slightly, his mouth sagging and his forehead wrinkling in thought.

"Unless?" the doctor probed.

Douglas stared at the floor, as though watching a scene play out in his mind.

"Inspector Brown?"

"I have to leave," he replied. "I'm sorry," he said, hurriedly gathering his coat and pushing his arms into the sleeves.

"Inspector Brown," the psychologist said in a firm voice. "I have not yet completed my evaluation. I cannot give your chief a clearance if—"

"—Yeah yeah," he answered, checking to make sure he hadn't left anything in his chair. "Whatever, doc. Tell Johnson anything you want, just tell him I'm ready and clear for duty."

"But Inspector Brown," the doctor sighed.

"I've got to...I...uh..." Douglas said, still looking around his space in a confused manner.

"Inspector Brown?"

"Alright. I'm good," Douglas decided. "Thanks," he added

without looking up and headed to the door.

"Inspector Brown!" the psychologist called. "I can't give you a clearance if—"

The door clacked shut and the doctor was all alone. He dropped his pen on the table beside him, then rose and walked to his desk. He pressed a button on his phone and muttered a curse.

"Yes, Dr. Sung?" the phone answered.

"Get ahold of Chief Inspector Johnson," he ordered. "And what does my afternoon look like?"

"You have a ten-fifteen, and then you are free for the next four hours, doctor," the woman on the speaker replied. "You have three appointments after two."

"I'm taking the afternoon for some personal business. Make arrangements for me to meet with Johnson at one-thirty," he requested.

"Yes, doctor," the line promised.

Dr. Sung pressed the end button and took a seat. He lifted the notes and studied them in the light from the window. There was a pattern here, he knew; a key to unlocking Douglas Brown. If he could crack this, he might not only be able to save this man from the maniac that was hunting him but perhaps he could assist in finding and capturing the maniac himself.

"Doctor?" the voice chirped on his phone.

Dr. Sung dropped the notepad on the desk and replied, "Yes?"

"You're ten-fifteen is here."

"Send him in," the doctor directed. He opened a drawer in his desk, tore from the yellow pad his notes for Douglas, and slid them into a file labelled: Brown, D – MPE.

The door to his office swung open and a tall, thin man walked in. He was clean-shaven, with weathered skin and red shoots of receding hair.

"Mr. Murphy?" the doctor said, rising from his seat. He walked around his desk and extended a hand. "I am Dr. Sung."

"It's a pleasure to meet you finally, doctor," the man replied in a thick British accent.

The wording made Dr. Sung cock his head to the side and eye the patient, smiling uncomfortably. "Have you heard of me?" the doctor inquired.

"I have," the man answered, taking the doctor's hand in a delicate grasp and giving it a slow shake. "You were highly recommended by a friend of mine at the police station."

"Oh?" the doctor responded. "And who would that be?"

"Jin Ma," the man answered directly.

"Jin Ma?" the doctor said, pulling his hand from Mr. Murphy's. "I don't remember a Jin Ma. Did I treat him?"

"Not exactly," the man answered.

Dr. Sung studied the figure for a moment and then offered, "Would you like to sit, Mr. Murphy?"

"Please," he said, "call me Richard."

"But I don't understand, Doug," Louise complained. "It just seems wrong."

Douglas tossed the overnight bag on the bed and moved to her dresser. "It's just not safe for you right now."

Louise watched as Douglas rifled through her drawers, tossing shirts, panties, shorts, and whatever else his hand touched first into the bag. "Doug?"

"Get your toiletries," he suggested. "You have to be ready to leave in a few minutes. I'll call a cab. Wait," he said in a sharp snap. "No. No calls. He'll have thought of that."

"What?" Louise asked. "Who?"

"Honey," he said with a bit of an edge in his voice. "Please just get moving."

"It's him, right?" she guessed. "It's that Richard Blythe, isn't it?"

"Louise," Douglas sighed, his tone growing irritated.

"You think he's going to hurt you?" she pressed.

"Not directly, I'm afraid."

"What does that mean?"

"It means," Douglas answered, raising his voice louder than he meant to, "that he is attacking those around me. He's calling his shots and cutting down those just on the edge of my reach. They are all getting closer and closer to my inner circle."

Her face flashed with a realization. "And I'm...?"

"At the centre of that circle," he confirmed. "I need you gone until this is over. Don't tell me where. Don't tell anyone. Don't go to family or friends. You need to disappear." He walked over and grasped his wife by the shoulders. "You can't be here."

"But you?"

"He isn't hunting me," Douglas said, almost believing himself. "He's torturing me, and you would be the ultimate target."

"But how will I know when to return?" she asked.

"Watch the news," Douglas replied. "When he's been caught, come home."

"Why can't I go to family? Or the police? Can't we put me in a safe house here in town?" she worried.

"No," Douglas said. "We can't trust the system. He's relying on us doing just that. You need to leave. There is an impounded car out front. Take it to another place. Rent a new car with cash. Drive that to another city and then get out. Pay cash. Find a hotel and rent a room somewhere. Stay low. Come home when it's all over."

"But..."

"Louise," Douglas pled. "I love you, but you will die if you stay."

He plucked the bag off the bed and pushed it into her arms. Pack your bathroom things and go. The sooner you leave the better your chances."

"I love you, Doug," she sputtered between tears.

"I'll be fine," he lied. "We'll all be fine."

8

London - 1982

Douglas stood at his desk, reading the two words scrawled on a blank postcard.

Look outside.

This can't be what it looks like, he thought to himself. The inspector felt his heart rate quicken and his temperature rise as the implications of the note began to sink in.

This was the bomber. There was no other explanation.

Douglas held the small piece of cardboard like a priceless relic, not wanting to damage it but not wanting to let it go either. It was the only correspondence anyone had received from the terrorist, and he knew full well the implications of such a piece of evidence. This could be the link. This could be the bomber's mistake. With this one little note, there just may be the opportunity to actually catch this man. But if the note was placed by the bomber then the bomber had been inside the police station. More than that, the bomber had been in the station within the last couple of hours, since there was no note there when Douglas had returned from lunch.

The cop in Douglas took over. He snatched up the envelope and turned to head off to the lab. If there was anything here that could lead him to the bomber, then he needed to know about it and there was no time to lose. The next bomb could be any day. Then Douglas froze.

Something inside stopped the inspector before he could take his first step. He thought of the investigation thus far, the way the case had been managed and his most recent complaints to his superintendent. Douglas thought of how he had followed every step, and every rule, and was rewarded with being ordered to take a leave of absence. If he handed this card over, how could he be assured that it would be investigated fully? There were procedures for evidence discovered during an investigation, but those same procedures had hobbled the agency and kept them several steps behind. If they checked everything out the way the agency was supposed to but couldn't find anything, it would most certainly hit some desk in the lab and die. The only connection between Douglas and the killer would find a home in a file and not move until the investigation was over and someone was writing the book.

"No," he swore aloud, refusing to accept that as an option. "No."

Douglas took a look around at his co-workers. Most had gone home except the few still intent upon their own tasks, working hard on their caseloads and trying to not be too distracted. From what he could tell, they had yet to notice him with the note.

This could be the break he needed, and with the next week off Douglas decided that he would be free to chase leads without the worry of following any sort of policy or procedure. He would be a regular citizen looking into a problem that affected everyone in the city. He would have every right to investigate however he saw fit since he would not be acting as a law enforcement officer. Suddenly, he felt a ray of hope in an otherwise hopeless case.

He turned and looked at his desk but found nothing else new or out of order. He flipped the note over, looking for a logo or an insignia; anything that might help him identify the source of the card. He read the words aloud, in a slow and careful voice, then considered what the note meant.

Why me? the inspector wondered.

From where he was, Douglas could not see the front of the station or the street. There were no windows around his desk, save for a few high, narrow openings which showed a sliver of the dark evening sky and the corner of a nearby building. If the bomber really had been the one to place the note, then he had done it on purpose. There had to be a reason for picking Douglas above everyone else, there were plenty of men and women working on this case. There had to be something.

Look outside.

Why pick someone without a view of the inner-city youth, without a clear view of the outside? Douglas just stood there for several moments, contemplating the note. With a few tentative movements, he glided to the hall and took several steps toward the front of the station. He paused when the front door came into view and stared out the window, studying the scene. Men and women walked by, and cars filled the busy street. All in all, it was a typical scene, just as he would have imagined it.

But something was pulling at him. It was as though a string was tied to his belly, and he was being slowly drawn to the door. Douglas searched the crowd outside, taking one quiet step after the next, head down and eyes narrowed. He eagerly scrutinized every face, hunting for anyone who was watching him. As Douglas reached the door, it finally hit him. He had been searching the crowds, hoping to see someone looking back at him; that was what he was trained to do.

As he reached the front door, Douglas looked for any item that might be out of place. He scanned cars and the sides of buildings. He looked over signs posted along the street. He then looked at the posts and spied something that made his breath catch in his throat. There, just a few feet from the station entrance was a pink concert poster hanging on a lamp post. Splattered across the front of the poster was the term 'Most Wanted', and a picture of Douglas. The notice was so bright he was ashamed that he had missed it at first, but it also blended in so completely with the rest of the surroundings that he could explain having never seen it if he wasn't looking. He reached out and peeled the advertisement from the post and read the details.

'One Night Only!' it read. 'See Douglas Brown Make History!'
Douglas looked around and took a deep breath.

'Friday the 11th at 8.15pm. The Old Kingsway Tram Tunnel.'

Douglas looked at his watch and gasped. It was 7.35 at that moment and it was the 11th. His heart froze for a beat. The Old Kingsway Tram Tunnel had been vacant for some years. The teenagers would break in and have parties occasionally, and there was plenty of vandalism, but other than that it had sat empty for years. It was isolated and would certainly be without security or traffic.

He would be alone. And yet, the bomber was calling out Douglas personally. Why? There were literally over forty people who were assigned to this case and this case alone. Douglas was just one face in that crowd. Why him?

He didn't allow much time to stew on that question. He had to make a choice and fast. What would he do with the note? It was most certainly an invitation to a trap, but did he follow procedure and notify his commander?

"What commander?" Douglas huffed and then ran back to his desk. He slipped by persons who looked at him queerly, and he nodded and apologised as he went, still rushing. Douglas reached his desk, grabbed his jacket and keys and then headed towards the exit.

"Doug?" a voice asked.

For a moment he considered ignoring it, but Douglas found himself turning to face his superintendent one more time.

"I trust you," Sheridan reminded him. "I think you are one of the best, but cases like this leave a mark. A deep one. I need to know that, after all of this, I'm still going to have one of the most talented investigators in London."

He knew what Sheridan was trying to say, but the wording was terrible. It sounded as though he only cared about protecting one of his assets, and Douglas said as much.

"In a way, yes," Sheridan admitted. "You are an extremely valuable employee and I do not want to lose such a gifted member of the staff, but there is more. You are an excellent man, Doug. I want to know that, when this is all over, you will still be the man you are. I care that you are well through this, and I want to be doing my part to keep you from being overwhelmed."

"You've caged one of your favourite dogs on the day of the hunt," Douglas remarked. "And, right now, all this dog lives for is finding this guy and ending this."

The superintendent's face, which only a moment before had held a sympathetic expression, was now growing hard and cold. "I will see you here in a week then," he replied, "and if this case is still open, I will put you right back to work. Until then, I need you to rest yourself."

"Right," Douglas snapped then stalked off quickly for his car.

At the door to the car park, Douglas looked down at his watch. He had thirty minutes to make the appointment. Thoughts pounded against his head. Would the bomb go off at eight-fifteen? Or was this just the appointment time when the bomber would introduce himself? What did the note mean by Douglas making history? Why was the bomber doing this? What did he have to gain from this? And why him?

He slipped behind the wheel of his car and started the engine. Whatever the reason, and whatever the thought, for good or for evil, Douglas was about to find out.

9

"I need the call logs from this morning!" Douglas hollered into his radio. "Have them delivered to my desk. I'll be there in ten."

"Copy 525," the dispatcher replied.

"That son of a bitch," Douglas muttered, clicking the microphone back into its seat.

The patrol car squealed around a corner and horns blared as he raced back to the office. The engine roared through the streets; cars whipped past, mere coloured blurs down both sides of the street. Douglas slammed on the brakes and slid around another corner, nicking the curb and causing the tires to skip angrily. By the time he screeched to a halt in his parking space, he was covered in sweat.

"What do you have?" Johnson demanded, catching him as he was stomping through the halls.

"It's so stupid," Douglas professed. "I should have had it checked first thing. The police log. Blythe picked the car and the spot. He had to have made the call."

"Doug?" Johnson interrupted.

"No, chief," Douglas defended, his breath coming in puffs as he hustled to his desk. "I know Blythe. He has to be in control. He would never have allowed the car to just wander around by chance."

"Doug?"

The two rounded the corner of what was storage but now served as the makeshift investigator's unit. "It has to be!" Douglas insisted. "He made the call."

"Douglas," Johnson said with a sharp edge in his tone. "We already checked that out."

They reached the desk as the words were spoken, and Douglas stared suspiciously at the folder on his desk.

"You were right," Johnson said, "in that it made sense to check it first. Within thirty minutes of the explosion, we had officers looking up the logs and tracing the calls. The caller that our car was responding to has been interviewed. It's not our guy. Before you ask," he added, holding up a hand, "we checked all of the callers that hour. There were seven," Johnson sighed, "all of which have been checked out and cleared. He didn't call, Doug."

"Then he pressured one of them, or created the reason for the call," Douglas asserted. "He's always in control."

"We found the source of the disturbance call," the chief inspector informed his detective. "He cleared out. Just some kid with a drum kit."

"No," Douglas said, shaking his head and screwing up his face. He snatched the folder off the desk and tore it open.

"Doug," his supervisor groaned.

"It can't be!"

"Maybe you need a break?" Johnson suggested.

The hair on Douglas' neck began to twist of its own accord and his ears burned. "What?" he asked in a venomous tone.

"You're stressed," Johnson pointed out.

"Officers are getting killed," Douglas reminded him in a dry, restrained voice. "It happens."

"But I need you on board."

Douglas closed his eyes and tried to pray that this wasn't

happening again.

"I haven't heard back from the doc yet," Johnson complained. "He hasn't cleared you, and I'm going to have to pull you if he doesn't get back to me soon."

"I just left there," Douglas explained. "He said I was good."

"Well he needs to tell me," Johnson said.

"Then call him and ask!" Douglas answered, louder than he intended.

"I'm scheduled to see him this afternoon. If he tells me you are cleared, then you may return to work. Otherwise," he said in a serious tone, "I need you off the clock."

It was all seeming too familiar to Douglas. "He's winning," the detective inspector shared. "Again. He's winning. And his next attack is any minute."

"Go home, Doug," Johnson said in a voice he hoped sounded understanding. "I'll call you this afternoon."

Douglas knew when to fight, but he also knew when to reorganise. He pulled his keys from his pocket, grabbed the call log, and turned to the door.

"Stay by a phone!" Johnson called out as Douglas pulled the back door open to the office and stepped into the lot.

His strides were long and full of purpose as he approached his ageing white Nissan Bluebird. The key clicked in the lock, the door squeaked open, and Douglas fell into the driver's seat. The door slammed closed and he hammered the dash with a yell. "Son of a bitch!" The engine revved to life and he pulled from the lot, determined that he wouldn't go home just yet. There had to be a lead. There had to be something he had missed. He decided that he would follow up on the call logs and see if he couldn't find something the others had missed.

And then he saw it, sitting there like it had always belonged in his car. Dropped on the floorboard of the passenger side was a black VHS without a label. At the next stop, Douglas bent down and scooped it up, flipping the cassette over, not at all surprised that it was totally blank on the outside.

"It's him."

The cars behind Douglas honked, irritated that he hadn't moved when the light turned green. He snapped out of his reverie and made a sharp left. He knew who had sent the tape, and there was no way he was handing this over just yet. He made for his house and prepared for the worst.

"Don't worry, my dear," the man whispered into Louise's hair. "It'll all be over soon."

10

Jin Ma hustled through his morning routine. The city felt like it was crawling under him, straining weakly to get away from the horror which had dropped upon Hong Kong. He couldn't help but feel a deep sense of responsibility to end this spree. He didn't know Blythe like Doug did, and he had no idea how long this would go on, but he knew, as an officer in the Royal Hong Kong Police Force, that it was his sworn duty to his family and country to protect them from terrorists like Blythe. There were few in the department who felt the urgency of that charge as strongly as Jin, and never more so than now. If Doug was right, this madman could continue unchecked for months if he chose to do so. There was no stopping him, and there was no predicting his next move. Blythe was an animal, and the only way to win was to beat him at his own game.

Jin hurriedly tied his shoes and then patted his pants pockets for his keys. Not finding them, he huffed a silent curse and stomped around the house anxiously. "Come on, come on, come on," he grumbled, searching every clear table and counter he passed. He checked his watch and gave a short growl. He had promised Johnson that he would be in first thing to go over the blast sites again. There had to be a connecting point between them so far, and if anything was missed they had to find it soon. Blythe would not wait long before he struck again. Doug said that they were not searching for a serial bomber, but a madman who fancied himself a revolutionist.

"He won't stick to bombs," Doug had said earlier. "He will use anything that can give him power over the city. It's all about fear and control. He feels like there is nothing we can do to stop him," Doug had added darkly, "and every move is another attempt to prove just that."

The words rattled around in his mind as the search for keys continued. Finally, Jin stopped, pressed his palms to the side of his head, and took a long, deep breath. "Where did I have them last?" he asked the room quietly, then sighed with the memory. Jin walked to the coat tree and gave his jacket a shake. It jingled back at him happily. The officer shook his head and yanked the jacket off the tree, scolding himself for not having his head together. Keys in hand, he whipped the front door open and stepped into the warm morning breeze.

Head down and mind racing, Jin make great strides down the side of his apartment building and out to the lot.

"Sir?" an old man called.

Jin waved and smiled but kept going. He didn't have time for some lost old man.

"Sir?" came the call again.

Jin rolled his eyes and waved again. "I'm sorry," he answered, his need for respecting his elders battling severely with his need to be on his way. "I really have to be going."

"Sir?" the old man called again, slowly moving towards Jin's car.

"Yes?" Jin asked harshly as he reached his car and shook his keys.

"I wouldn't do that, sir," the old man cautioned.

The jingling stopped and Jin squinted at the stranger. "What did you say?" he demanded, studying the figure before him. He would be tall if he wasn't hunched over. A long coat with many panels hung loosely over his shoulders, and a cap with a large bill was pressed down over his forehead.

"There was a man messing with that car," the older gentleman declared. "He wasn't there for long, but he had a bag with him."

Jin's heart raced and the keys began to shake again. "Who was he?" Jin demanded. "Was he English? What did he look like?"

"He looked," the old man said, coming closer. "He looked…" The man brushed his coat aside to reveal a pistol levelled at Jin. "He looked like me," the old man confessed.

The officer's hand twitched but the old man cut him off.

"Ah, ah, ah," he warned. "Do it and die."

"Who are you?" Jin snapped.

"Like you don't know," the man answered, dropping his Chinese accent and stretching his jaw.

"Blythe," Jin announced.

"Hello, Officer Ma," he answered. "Let's go for a ride."

The blindfold was carefully, almost lovingly, peeled from Jin's face. The officer looked around and then sighed.

"You know how this is going to work, don't you?" Blythe asked.

Jin didn't need the situation explained. He was in a basement of some kind, complete with block walls and a washed concrete floor. It was newer construction as far as he could tell, but then again there were so many new buildings cropping up all over the city that face would hardly matter. If this ended the way Jin imagined, Blythe would need it to be soundproof or at least not full of people. Best bet was some large office building after hours, buried a few floors down.

Blythe smiled and Jin gauged whether or not he could spit on his captor over the distance between them. The Englishman stood almost four meters away with a clear plastic curtain behind him and a video camera to his right. Jin pulled against his bonds and found himself tied and strapped to a chair.

"I've turned the camera on," Blythe began.

"I know what you want," Jin assured him.

Unfazed, Blythe continued, "You will tell your friends at the station to come and save you."

"I will not," the officer promised.

"Do what I ask," Blythe pressed on, "and I will let you walk. Refuse..."

"You're going to kill me anyway," Jin said, glaring with a burning hostility at the terrorist.

"Really I don't plan to," Blythe assured him. "I will be just as happy letting you go."

"Then why should I ask to have them come save me, hmm?" Jin asked. "If I'll be free anyway?"

"Because," Blythe answered with a smile. "Obviously you're not the one I wanted."

"Doug," Jin guessed.

"He is a unique character," the Englishman admitted.

Jin narrowed his eyes and asked, "Why? What is it about him? Why are you doing this?" His eyes dropped to the pistol in Blythe's hand, knowing that there was only one way this could end. Jin might as well get some answers before it was over.

"Doug," Blythe sang, giving the name an obscene number of syllables. "He's not like you. He's not like any of you. He was dark, and alone, and pained, and dead. I brought him to life. In London, I dragged Douglas from the pit that was slowing stealing his life and raised him to the position of a god. He was immortal when he hunted me. Ah, you should have seen it," Blythe sighed, reminiscing and looking off into the corner of the room. "The fire that rose in his belly and burned in his eyes. I was Doctor Frankenstein and Inspector Brown was my monster. From death I drew him and, as the story foretold, he turned against me."

"He sent you to prison," Jin agreed.

The laughter that spilt from Blythe was low and sick and dreadful. "You don't understand, Officer Ma. He was supposed to send me to prison. That wasn't the betrayal."

Jin furrowed his brow and wracked his mind.

"The moment I was gone," Blythe continued, "Douglas died again. He's only alive with me, and the only way he can help me change the world is if he is alive."

"You're a madman," Jin accused.

"You are a man of little vision," Blythe returned. "That's why you're tied to a chair, and Douglas will change the world. Now," he announced, "you will tell them to come to you – to rescue you – or I will kill you, Ma."

"You're planning to kill us all in the end anyway," Jin answered. "I have no intention of helping you do it."

The pistol weighing Blythe's hand bobbed as he flexed his fingers around the grip. "I don't want to kill any of you," he promised. Jin snorted but Blythe ignored him. "Aren't you listening to me? I need Douglas. I need him to help me change the world. I don't care if you live or die, Ma. You are a spot on the world that men like Doug will burn away. Ask for help," the Englishman again offered, "and you will walk out of here."

Jin ground his teeth and again pulled upon his ropes.

"And this isn't television, remember," Blythe said, looking for the record button on the camera. "If we fail this take I'll just do it again. So," he said, staring the camera, "ready?"

11

Douglas pressed play on the VCR and regretted it immediately.

"Jin?" Douglas' voice was so clogged with shock that the name came out as more of a choke than a word.

"Ready?" a voice off-camera asked.

The small officer shifted in his seat and stared at the ground.

Douglas stood there in his living room, watching his friend and coworker strain against his bonds.

"Is there something you would like to tell your friends at the police station?" the voice asked.

Jin shuttered and swallowed a cough. "Do not come for me," he managed.

"Now Mr. Ma," the voice scolded lightly. "That is not what we—"

"—Do not come for me," Jin demanded into the camera.

Douglas quickly scanned the room in the scene, but he couldn't make much out. There was a cinderblock wall behind him, painted white, and the floor was not visible. The lights hummed and there was an echo in the room, but that didn't really help him pick one basement location over any other.

"Where are you?" Douglas demanded of the television.

"If you are watching this," Jin said in cold certainty, "then I am dead anyway."

"Tell me where you are!" Douglas demanded of the tape.

70

"And that means you too, Doug," Jin said, staring right into the lens. "Find this son of a bitch, but don't plan on finding me."

Douglas shivered at the mention of his name.

"By now, I'm dead," the officer insisted.

"Don't you want to be saved, Mr. Ma?" the voice asked.

It was Blythe. There was no other explanation.

"Don't you want to live?" the kidnapper asked.

"I want you to die," Jin said coldly, staring to the left of the camera.

"Well then," Blythe replied coolly, "if it is not salvation you hope for..."

A pistol appeared on the left side of the screen.

Fire burst from the end of the barrel and Jin flinched under his bonds. The officer screamed as a red streak poured from below his right lung. Another explosion rang out and Jin wailed in his chair.

"No!" Douglas roared. "You fuck! You fucking son of a bitch! No!"

Jin cried, his breath coming in heaves and sighs. Blood stained his lap and ran down the legs of his pants. Douglas fell to his knees and stared at the screen, shock crippling him from any other response.

"Help," Jin mumbled through the spit dumping over his bottom lip. "Help."

"And now you want to be saved?" Blythe asked with a sneer. The gun bobbed with the question before cracking one last time. The side of Jin's head disappeared and the wall behind him was painted with a shot of bright red.

The television popped and the screen became blue. Douglas fell to his side and wept into the carpet. His body seemed to lose all shape as he lay there, without any sense of hope or direction. The clock could have turned minutes or hours; he didn't know how long he had been there, the devastation he felt after seeing what he had just witnessed was so complete. Eventually, the phone rang and the machine picked up.

"Doug? It's Christopher. I need you to call me back right away. And see if you can't get Jin on the line. He's been out of the office since this morning and I need him at the station. Bye."

The television hummed back at Douglas with its unflinching blue face, and eventually, the shock became numbness. It wasn't long before the phone rang again.

"Dammit, Doug. It's Johnson. Answer your phone. You better be home and not..."

Douglas lifted the receiver and pressed the speaker to his ear.

"Brown," he said softly.

"Doug?" Johnson stated in a surprised tone. "I need you back at the station."

"No."

"What?"

Douglas looked back at the screen, still shining blue, and shook his head. "I said no."

"Doug," Johnson said in a forced tone, "When did you last see Dr. Sung?"

Ice rattled in Douglas' fingertips.

"You said you had just left him when I saw you," Johnson clarified, "but when did you actually see him last? Do you remember the time?"

"What the hell does it matter?" Douglas snapped.

"Because he's dead," Johnson replied. "He was killed in his office sometime today, and we think it may have been Blythe."

Douglas' head swam and he felt as though he might collapse again. He steadied himself on a nearby chair and worked hard at breathing.

"If you're not up to this, I understand," Johnson assured him. "But I need Jin. Have you seen him?"

Douglas looked back at the blue screen.

"He's dead," he whispered into the receiver.

The other end of the line went silent.

"Blythe took him, held him hostage, and executed him," Douglas explained in a monotonous drone.

"How do you know this?" Johnson demanded in a breathless voice.

"Because the bastard videotaped it," Douglas said, feeling the sob rise in his throat, "and the sick fuck sent me the tape."

"We have to get you out of there," Johnson said suddenly. "We need you here at the station, where you're safe."

Douglas stood there rigid with the phone pressed to his ear.

"If he's killing cops, why is he sending you the tape?" Johnson asked rhetorically. "You aren't safe, Doug."

"No one is," the detective inspector replied, and hung up the phone.

Douglas walked around the room, a hand curved and digging frantically at his scalp. He stomped past the VCR with the tape still buried within and cut a line to the front door of his small house. He stepped outside and moved to go down the front steps but his legs quit when his eyes scanned the walkway. Positioned in the middle of the narrow path was a potted bamboo plant, and nestled amongst the shining green stalks was a bulky manila envelope with a single word scrawled in black marker: Tag.

Douglas walked uncertainly down the steps and toward the plant, his eyes cutting up and down the street though he was positive he would find no other sign of him. The inspector burned within, knowing that there was nothing in the bag that he wished to find, but that if he wanted to find Blythe he would have to open it eventually. He knelt beside the plant and examined the envelope. It was larger than a typical business letter and it looked like it contained a box of some kind.

His head swam with possibilities. Plastic explosives? A detonator? Whatever was in there, Douglas was confident that he didn't want it.

The inspector gently pinched the corner of the envelope between his fingers and lifted it out of its cradle. It was heavy in his hand and lopsided in its package. Douglas held the item up and looked at all sides, finding that Blythe had written "Open Me" over the sealed flap. Douglas carefully set the package on the walkway and covered his eyes behind a hand.

"What am I doing?" he wondered to himself. "I blow up, and he's gone forever. But—" he sighed with resignation "—Louise is safe, and I am running out of time."

Douglas pulled a pocketknife out of his pants and clicked the blade open. He scratched the top of the envelope just enough to open it and used the point of the blade to spread the paper. Leaning over, he glanced inside the envelope.

"Nǐ hǎo!"

Douglas jumped back at the loud announcement and stared wide-eyed at Yun, the neighbourhood boy who had visited him so often over the past months.

"Nǐ hǎo!" the boy said again, a happy expression splattered over his face.

Douglas' mind went blank. He tried to remember how to say, "Run away before you die," but all he could manage was a scowl and a wave. The boy looked at him with a confused face until Douglas again flagged him away. The boy turned sadly and backed off as far as the street. Douglas wiped his face and decided that would have to be as good as it got.

Tipping his head back to the package, Douglas peered inside and knit his brow at the sight. It was a dark grey plastic box with a small black nob at one end. Douglas cut the paper around the box and chuckled darkly when he recognized what it was.

"Son of a bitch," he muttered.

A cell phone.

Douglas pulled at the little flap covering the buttons and stared at the device. His heart lurched when the numbers and screen lit up and the phone chirped loudly at him. He took a breath, extended the antenna, and pressed the Talk button.

"Hello, Detective Inspector," Blythe said in a in a tone that reeked of self-satisfaction. Ready to play one last time?"

12

London – 1982

Douglas looked at his watch and frowned. The face read 8:16, and Douglas wondered if he hadn't missed his chance. One voice deep within told him to turn around. The voice demanded that he call for backup, establish a perimeter, and close the noose on this psychopath. Then another voice broke in. "One Night Only!" the voice cried out. "See Douglas Brown Make History!" Douglas pulled into a side street off the busy Kingsway road and found a parking space near the location. He reached underneath his seat and pulled out the Glock 17 he had been issued since the bombing crisis had hit the capital and checked the 9×19mm Parabellum cartridge, securing it to the underside of the handle with a slap of his palm. He placed the pistol in his inside jacket pocket and then fumbled around for a small torch, flipped the slide button to check it and then hauled himself out of the vehicle.

The sound of his car door shutting echoed off the neighbouring buildings and he stood for a moment, breathing in the early evening air. He walked back onto the main road and picked up his pace as he approached the underpass that had been used for double-decker trams until 1953 and then for cars between Waterloo Bridge and the Aldwych until its closure.

Douglas stood at the locked gates at the start of the underpass for a moment, peering through to the dark tunnel beyond, which itself was protected by a steel grid. He looked around as if steeling himself for what might lay ahead, and then grabbed the rusty metal bars and hauled himself upwards. He positioned his feet on the metal, pushing himself up to the top, and then manoeuvred at a slower pace to avoid the spikes at the top. His feet slipped and he nearly lost his balance but regained composure just as fast. He really needed to work out more, he thought. Once over, it was an easy descent and he was soon walking slowly down the sloping underpass, between ageing grey walls and the black metal railings that ran along the top of them. He moved slower now, his eyes transfixed on the tunnel entrance ahead.

It wasn't too late to turn back.

The entrance had a black metal grid with a gated doorway that had been padlocked, except it had been cut and lay discarded on the ground, the door inched open. Douglas took his Glock 17 out of his jacket pocket and slipped into the darkness.

Despite not being able to see very well, Doug could feel the extent of the tunnel that seemed to reach onwards into the gloom. An echo dripping from the ceiling grew louder as he slowly made his way further into the tunnel. He could feel the original tram lines and unused electrical conduits under his feet that once led to the old Aldwych station.

He couldn't sense that there was anyone there. Maybe it was a hoax, some idiots playing games? He took out his torch, switched it on to get an idea of his bearings. The torchlight revealed a batch of road signs stacked against the wall and road construction material that had obviously been stored there and the indents on the wall from advertising boards that had long been removed.

Douglas stood on the threshold, studying the darkness. He couldn't see anything, but there was a faint noise in the air. It was a muffled sound, like an animal trapped in a sack or a voice crying out through water.

"Oh shit," Douglas muttered, and, as if waiting for its cue, a generator erupted into life, powering a tree of spotlights. The tunnel was bathed in a harsh, yellow glow and the quiet roar of the small motor. Parked at the other end of the tunnel was a single-level transit bus, and dividing the distance between the bus and Douglas was a little girl in a white and pink church dress, swathed in lace and ruffles. At her feet were a teddy bear and a wide-brim hat, apparently dropped haphazardly and now resting just as they had fallen. The child was blindfolded, though that did not stop the tears from soaking through the material and running down both cheeks. The girl could not have been more than eight or nine years old, and her body shook vigorously under the hum of the lights.

As Douglas' eyes finally adjusted to the light, he quickly took in his surroundings. There was a prefabricated building on the right side, in line with a series of square pillars, that was a recess used as a dumping ground for more unused street signs.

Douglas took a step toward the child, shushing her lovingly but fully aware that someone had activated the generator. His hand flexed around the grip of his weapon and he prepared for the ambush. There was no point in asking a blindfolded child where her captor was, but Douglas hoped he might be able to free her before the bomber made his formal appearance.

The muffled noises suddenly grew louder, and Douglas stared at the child in wonder. She wasn't gagged, and he could hear her rough breathing and tiny sobs clearly from where he stood. When his eyes followed the sound to the source, the detective let out a long moan. Behind the windows of the bus were the faint outlines of dozens of persons. Their heads were all hidden behind sacks, and undoubtedly they were all tied to their seats.

"Welcome!" called a loud voice from behind the spotlights.

"Welcome! Though," the voice added in a hurt tone, "you are a little late. That will have an effect on our little arrangement here."

Douglas wheeled toward the sound and levelled his firearm at the dark corner behind the lamps. Unable to see the figure, Douglas felt foolish and exposed, though he held his position and gritted his teeth. "Who are you?" he demanded in a voice he hoped sounded commanding.

"Oh, the clichés!" the voice cried, the sounds of which reverberated in the wide expanse. "Always with the clichés! This is your moment, Doug! Your chance! Every word you speak and every move you make from the moment you found the poster until this is all over will be scrutinized, analyzed, and shared as an example of outstanding police work for decades to come!" Douglas couldn't tell if the bomber was being sarcastic, or if he was always this excited, but his host did not give much time for debating that point. "Here you stand," he continued, "at the crossroads of a historic event, and look at you! Pointing a gun at nothing and reciting tired lines from action movies. You should be ashamed!"

Douglas kept his pistol pointed to where he thought the voice was originating, though he let his eyes drift to the sides, looking for any sign of movement or hint of the bomber.

"But never fear," the voice called out, now off to the right of the lights. "History is written by those who live long enough to tell it. Play your hand wisely, and you can write this scene however you choose."

"What's your name?" Douglas demanded.

"My name is Blythe," the darkness answered. "Richard Blythe. And if you want to make it to the end of the game," he warned, "you will drop your weapon and slide it out of your reach."

Douglas' hand tightened around the grip, pressing the moisture from his hand and causing a slight tremble in the barrel.

"You are already late," Blythe reminded him. "You really have no more time to lose. That bus has one last stop to make, and if you want to save anybody tonight you should drop that gun straight away."

"Show me your face," Douglas ordered.

"Drop your weapon," Blythe replied venomously, "or I kill the child."

The little girl shook wildly and the tears pressed their way under the blindfold, though she remained right where Blythe had placed her.

"Drop-Your-Weapon," Blythe instructed, pronouncing each word with a strained intensity.

"Please," the girl whispered.

Douglas felt torn and his grip loosened at the tiny plea.

"Time is ticking by, Douglas!" Blythe cried.

"Please, sir," the child continued. "Don't let him kill me."

The barrel lowered until the gun was hanging limply at the detective's side. His knees wobbled a little as he bent, dropping the sidearm onto the concrete floor.

"Very good, Douglas," Blythe cheered in a patronizing voice. "Now kick it away."

"I am going to tear you to shreds," Douglas promised, sending the pistol clattering into shadow.

"Good," Blythe said, stepping from the left of the lamps and smiling widely at the detective. He was thin, and tall, with a wild bush of red hair perched atop his head and eyes that looked green in the obscure light. "Ready to make history?"

Douglas growled and took a step toward the bomber.

"The bus is laden with explosives," Blythe announced calmly.

"I am going to kill you," Douglas promised.

Blythe just smiled all the more then said, "And the child is the trigger."

Douglas stopped cold and looked at the girl's feet. A wire ran from under a polished white shoe in a straight line to the bus.

"Oh shit."

"There is a timer on the bus," Blythe pressed on. "Find it and stop the bomb, and we all live. Save the girl, and everyone on that bus dies."

Douglas' mind flooded and crashed. He just had to trace the wire and deactivate the device somehow, but he had no experience with explosives and couldn't imagine the first step to stopping a timer short of ripping it out. It couldn't always be like the movies. If the timer was removed that wouldn't set off the bomb, would it?

"Tick, tick, tick!" Blythe said, almost singing happily. "The letter's in the mail and the sand is slipping through the glass. You now have forty-five seconds."

"What?!?" Douglas panted.

"I told you to be here at a quarter past," Blythe reminded him. "This clock has been running for thirty minutes, and that child looks mighty tired. If she comes off that trigger, then it's all over for those poor people on the bus. Not to mention we are dangerously close as well. Who knows? We all might die!" he added with a twisted giggle. "Thirty-five seconds."

A light flashed in the detective's brain. Douglas raced to the little girl and unbuckled her shoe. Pressing the sole to the floor, Douglas yanked the child's foot free and stepped on the empty shoe. Blythe sucked wind excitedly before disappearing suddenly behind the prefab building. Douglas tore the blindfold from the girl's eyes and yelled, "Run!"

The child just stood there, terrified.

"Run!" he boomed in her face.

"But he'll kill me," the child declared in a quiet, wavering voice.

The tunnel was suddenly filled with light and sound and smoke and debris. Douglas' ears rang viciously and his eyes bulged, his body thrown backwards through the air before hitting the ground hard. The skin of his arms and neck burned as he pushed himself from the ground and looked at the burning bus. Suddenly the tunnel felt like a furnace. A series of screams punctured the air as the frame snapped and popped, with most of the roof blown clean off the vehicle.

The girl.

Douglas turned back to find the body of the child lying beside him. He pulled himself to her and touched her face. "Hey," Douglas said quietly. "Hey. Are you alright?"

Blythe began laughing from somewhere Douglas couldn't see, like someone gone insane.

"Can you hear me? Little girl! Can you hear me?"

"He's..." she sputtered quietly, opening her eyes a crack. "He's killing me," she said finally.

"You're fine," Douglas promised, tears pressing against the corners of his eyes. "You're fine."

"He's killing me," she repeated, the sound of Blythe's laughter, echoing against the crackling flames, making for a terrifying soundtrack to the moment.

"No, sweetie," Douglas said, brushing hair from her forehead. "You're fine," he insisted, tucking a lock behind her ear. "You're..." His words died in the air, and Douglas' hand froze behind the child's ear. A hard, sharp edge met his fingertip, and when Douglas pulled his hand back it was covered in blood. He grimaced and pulled the hair away from the wound. "No," he gasped, horrified by the sight. "Fuck!"

A piece of sheet metal had wedged itself in her neck, and blood was streaming over the projectile. A large, red pool was growing under her head, enough that her hair was soon losing its colour in the sticky mess.

The child's body flexed, then deflated under Douglas' hand. Tears fell freely over the body of the little girl until Douglas backed away, pushing himself to his feet.

Laughter.

The detective was ignited by rage. He walked over to the blackened prefab building and stood in the doorway looking down at the curled frame of the murderer, where he had taken refuge from the blast. The pale-faced figure looked up and said with a smirk, "The letter's in the mail."

Douglas grabbed Blythe by the shirt and began punching him in the face for all he was worth, punching until the smirk was no more but a bloodied, bruised pulp.

13

Hong Kong

Douglas stood tall in the walkway, phone pressed tightly against his ear. "I will find you, you twisted son of a bitch," he promised. "I will find you and I will kill you where you stand."

"I look forward to you trying," Blythe answered in a lighthearted tone. "But first," he laughed, clearly enjoying the moment he had waited for, "there are a few surprises hidden around the city. Big surprises. The kind that leave a mark."

Douglas ground his teeth and turned his back to the boy still standing in the street. "I'm listening."

"The first detonator has been tucked safely away on Victoria Peak. Get to it in the next forty minutes, and you will be saving a lot of lives. Good luck, Detective Inspector Brown."

The phone chirped a single note and the buttons went dark. Douglas wheeled around once, ran into the house, and emerged a moment later with a pistol on his hip and a look of murderous determination on his face. He raced to his car and tore onto the streets. He wove through traffic like a man possessed, diving in and out of cars and pedestrians, honking and cursing out the window until he made it out of the city and through the Eastern Harbour Tunnel to Hong Kong Island.

The traffic condensed again as soon as Douglas was on the island, and it only worsened the closer he was to the peak.

Then Douglas got an idea.

The detective inspector cut a hard left and split a busy intersection. Cars around him honked and swerved, avoiding him but crashing into one another. Douglas didn't care a bit. Insurance would cover the drivers, and their inconvenience was nothing when compared to the damage that Blythe could commit with another bomb.

Douglas sped up as he approached his goal, jamming on the brakes and sliding to a stop before the office of the Peak Cable Car Company. He jumped out of the car and ran into the office, sliding past the front desk and cutting out the back door. Voices behind him erupted in protest but he ignored them. He ran up the platform and flagged down a conductor who was about to close the hatch on a car and start the ascent to the top of the peak.

"Stop!" Douglas cried. "Tíngzhǐ! Tíngzhǐ!"

The conductor eyed him with a worried expression but held the door.

"Police!" Douglas declared, holding up his badge.

"We full," the man explained apologetically in broken English.

Behind Douglas came a string of angry employees, all calling for him to stop at once. Douglas turned and showed the men his badge, then explained to the conductor, "I have to get to the Peak right now."

"I very sorry sir," the conductor began, but Douglas cut him off.

"Bomb!" the detective screamed. "There is a bomb!"

Immediately the car began to empty. Riders pushed and shoved to get out of the car while some spat anxious questions.

"Here? A bomb on the car?"

"On the peak?"

"What is he saying?"

Douglas screamed above the din, "There is a bomb, and the only way to stop it is to get me to the top of the peak right now!"

The stragglers jumped from the cable car and Douglas stepped in. He and the conductor exchanged a look for a moment, one raising his eyes in anticipation while the other stood there shaking and confused.

"Move!" Douglas bellowed. "Get this thing going before the bomb goes off."

The conductor slammed the door closed and threw the switch. The car lifted from the ground and took off into the air, bobbing from the pair of wires overhead. Douglas looked at his watch and began to second-guess his decision. There were twenty-eight minutes left, but would that be enough time to locate the bomb and disarm it before time ran out?

Douglas took out the cell phone and eyed the screen. The device sat there in his hand, as lifeless as a stone. The detective could hear the voice of Blythe in his head, and the mocking edge in his words. A snivelling sound drew his eyes up and to the conductor, who was now watching Douglas carefully and shaking freely.

"Don't worry," Douglas said in a determined voice. "We're going to kill this bastard."

The car crept over the city and above the trees. It rolled at a steady pace, climbing as it dipped and bounced on the cables. The conductor held the control, as though afraid of what the crazed policeman in the car might do. Douglas tried not look at his watch and instead took several deep breaths.

"Does it go any faster?" he asked, at last, unable to contain himself.

The man looked at Douglas repentantly and said, in his struggling English, "Very Sorry. This is fast. No more fast."

"As fast as it goes, huh?" Douglas said, watching the mountain grow in the window of the car. He took a deep breath and felt every second on his climb to the top.

Up the line was another car slowly making its way along the cables. The ride was a popular tourist attraction and thousands of people filed in and out of the cars in a year-round stream, but in that moment Douglas was lamenting each and every one of them. He could just make out the faces of the people in the car ahead of his when the conductor suddenly pulled the break.

The car rocked forward and swung back like a pendulum trying to find the centre.

"What the hell are you doing?" Douglas barked, holding on to the rail to avoid falling over. "We have to go."

The young man pointed up the line and made a worried face. "No," was all he said.

"There is a bomb about to blow up!" Douglas reminded him. "We can't just sit here and wait it out."

"No," the conductor replied, shrugging his shoulders to a comical height. Again he pointed up the line, then held his open hands' inches apart.

"We're too close to the other car?" Douglas guessed.

The conductor moved his hands another notch closer to one another and then dropped them both suddenly.

"Shit!" Douglas snapped, swinging a fist into the air. He pulled out the cell phone and looked at the dead screen, hating Blythe with every ounce he had left. Another glance at his watch and he realized that he had only twenty minutes left. He squeezed the phone in his hand and roared like some insane animal. The conductor blanched at the display, recoiling a little further into his corner while Douglas spun a circle and jammed the phone into his pocket.

The car rocked suddenly as the conductor drove them on and Douglas began breathing again. For the rest of the ascent, the young man never took his eyes off the control. Like a boy trapped in a cage with a tiger, it was as though he was afraid the slightest look could trigger a reaction with the beast in the car.

Normally, Douglas would have appreciated the tension in the car, but at that moment nothing compared with the drive he felt to cause as much harm to Blythe as he could. Something inside of him was stirring, and, frankly, the boy was right to be afraid.

The car up the line reached the landing platform and Douglas could feel the conductor increase the speed, eager to pacify the impatient cop. The rest of the trip seemed lightning fast compared to the first half, and in no time Douglas was pounding on the door and demanding out, even before they had reached the landing. The conductor happily obliged and opened the door at the detective's first request. As soon as he thought the fall wouldn't hurt him, Douglas slipped out of the car with a hop and stumbled a short distance before his feet found themselves. Balance restored, Douglas sprinted for the pavilion.

People were crowded in from one corner to the next, making it difficult to move quickly or see much at once. Anxiety snaked up his gut and fastened itself tightly around Douglas' lungs.

Eighteen minutes.

Douglas turned in a circle and fought the hopelessness trying to swallow him. He would need a fifty-man team to cover the entire area, and he was all alone. People milled about as if nothing was strange or out of the ordinary at all; as if there wasn't a madman holding death above their heads, primed and ready to release it at any moment. Douglas spun again and cried out in frustration.

Most of the persons at the pavilion stopped and stared, while the men and women who were closest to Douglas sped up and moved away. One of the men who had stopped to watch the grown man howling into the sky was a man in a tan jumpsuit. In one hand he held a black bag, and in the other was a manila envelope with a single word scrawled on the side.

Tag.

"Wait!" Douglas screamed, pointing at the man and running towards him. The maintenance worker took an involuntary step back before Douglas announced himself. "Police!" The detective pulled out his badge and held it in the air.

Some of the tourists made relieved expressions, but most still look terrified and confused. The maintenance employee dropped the bag and the envelope, the latter clacking loudly to the ground.

"No!" Doug screamed, quickening his pace.

He fell to a stop beside the envelope; his knees grinding into the gravel path. He looked carefully at the little yellow packet and thought it looked remarkably similar to the one outside his front door. *Another phone?* he wondered silently, but his attention was pulled from the package when the noise of the crowd swelled back into focus.

Douglas looked around at the mob, now forming a circle around him and slipped his badge onto his belt. "Get back!" he ordered. "Get back, now!"

Few people moved, and the lack of response was infuriating.

"Bomb!" Douglas screamed. "Bomb!"

It was a word the city had heard too often lately, and the response was everything Douglas thought it would be. The crowd scattered like wildfire, pouring towards the exit paths to the car park and the station. Screaming voices and stomping feet matched the throbbing in Douglas' head as he turned his attention back to the envelope.

Out of patience and running low on time, Douglas pried back the flap and turned the opening toward his face. Inside he found a black box with a protected trigger on one side. He pulled the detonator out and held it in his hand.

The cell phone rang so suddenly and loudly in his pocket that Douglas nearly dropped the detonator in fright. He scrambled to pull out the phone and to quickly answer it.

"Sixteen minutes left," Blythe reminded him.

"So you've brought me here," Douglas huffed, his breath running low. "I have the detonator. Now what?"

"Police!" a man called behind Douglas. The detective turned slowly with the phone pressed to his ear and the detonator in the other hand. Douglas found a chubby patrol officer with pistol drawn and levelled at his chest.

"Now is the real fun," Blythe explained.

The officer ordered Douglas to drop the phone and the device and to get on the ground. Douglas pinched the phone with his shoulder and showed his empty hand. He then slowly pulled his jacket open to reveal his badge firmly clipped to his belt. The patrol officer still barked for him to put the device down.

"There is a bomb on bus number 203," Blythe said lightly. "And for goodness sakes tell that beat cop to put his gun away before he hurts someone."

Douglas pulled the phone from his ear and raised his hands for the patrolman to see. "I am Detective Inspector Brown, of the Royal Hong Kong Police Force."

The patrolman lowered his weapons slightly but did not seem ready to walk away just yet.

"I am investigating the bombings, and I am working at the very moment to locate the next device," Douglas continued. "Now lower your weapon and help me secure the area."

Still, the policeman refused to move.

Like a whisper on the wind, Douglas could hear the voice of Blythe counting down the moments.

"A bus is going to explode any minute if I do not stop it," Douglas said, pleadingly. "Lower your weapon. Call central. Do whatever the fuck you want but I have a whole lot of people to save."

Douglas pushed the phone back to his ear stared defiantly at the officer.

"Nicely handled," Blythe praised as the patrolman stowed his weapon and put in a call on his radio. "Although time is quickly slipping by."

"So cut to it," Douglas ordered. "Where's the bus?"

"Yau Ma Tei," Blythe said lightly.

Douglas immediately scoffed. "That's twenty-five minutes away."

"And?" Blythe asked.

"I have fourteen minutes left," Douglas panted.

"Here's the deal, Detective," Blythe explained. "The bomb is set to go off when it reaches the school. If it does it will kill hundreds of people, most of them children."

"No," Douglas panted. "You sick asshole."

"You have the power to stop that from happening though," Blythe assured him.

The patrolman tapped Douglas on the shoulder and gave him a thumbs-up, as though to say he was all checked out. Douglas turned his back on the man and pressed the phone even more tightly to his ear.

Blythe continued in a casual voice. "Just set off the bomb now."

The words collided with Douglas' chest like a stream of bullets. "What?"

"Set it off now and you kill what, nine, maybe eleven people?" Blythe explained. "If that bus reaches the school it will be far worse. There were only eight students scheduled to be on the bus right now. You might get a few on the street, but all in all, you will be saving the lives of hundreds more. The choice is simple, Detective." Blythe's excited breath washed over the receiver on his end. "Just push the button."

Douglas froze.

"It's the only choice," Blythe insisted. "Kill a few, or do nothing and watch a school go up in flames. Your choice."

The phone beeped and went dead in Douglas' hand.

"Detective?" asked the patrolman.

Douglas turned around and stared off over the bay, across the hundreds of jutting skyscrapers that lay below and the mainland across Victoria Harbour.

"Detective?" the chubby police officer asked a second time.

The word seemed to snap Douglas back to life. He spun quickly and dropped the detonator down the front of his shirt. He then grabbed the officer's radio and ripped it off the man's belt. The patrolman screamed a protest, but Douglas was already running for the car park.

Cars were still crowding the exits, trying to escape the peak and the bomb threat. Douglas split his way through the cars until he saw his prize.

A motorcyclist was picking his way through the cars. Douglas ran up and grabbed the rider by the helmet. He peeled back until the man fell backwards over the rear tire.

"Police emergency," Douglas explained.

Without a rider, the bike lurched and smacked into a small pickup. Douglas picked up the bike, restarted it, and screamed through the press of vehicles like a suicidal maniac. He cut over grass and between trees, slipping and sliding his way down the hill and diving between cars as he went. Once Douglas found a spot of open road, he lifted the radio to his lips.

"525 to any unit in Yau Ma Tei," he cried. "This is a code 33 emergency. I need school bus 203 stopped and emptied before it reaches the school. Call the bus company. Call the school. Find out where it's going and stop it before it gets there. There is a 4-12 on the bus. I repeat, a 4-12."

Douglas dropped the radio down his shirt and opened the throttle. He cut through the city streets like a man on fire, diving between posts and parked cars and roaring down the straightaways. He made the Cross-Harbour Tunnel and drove in, the sound of the motorcycle's engine screaming loudly in the confined space. The bike slipped through the cars and around the toll booth, causing panic with the collectors but gaining a clear road ahead as he streaked toward the mainland.

On the other side, Douglas pulled out the radio and checked the time.

Three minutes.

"525," he barked into the microphone. "Does anyone have the bus?"

Douglas' heart skipped terribly as he waited a small eternity for a response.

"922," a patrol responded. "We have the bus and are unloading it now. Wylie and King's Park Rise."

"Evacuate the area, 922!" Douglas commanded. "You have just over one minute!"

Douglas held his breath as the seconds clicked by. When the explosion happened, it still caught him off guard. The sound tore through the city, shaking windows and rattling the ground for kilometres. A small ball of fire could be made out at the base of King's Park Rise, followed by a thick plume of smoke. Douglas whipped the motorcycle back to life and dashed to the scene.

When he arrived, he found the smouldering remains of a school bus and a burned-out police car. People were running in the street trying to get away, and officers were herding people who were injured or unable to walk alone.

The detective slipped off the bike and assessed the damage. The bus had been stopped along a retaining wall, the stones of which seemed to take the brunt of the blast. A patrol car had been parked at the nose of the bus and was currently burning freely. Douglas turned a circle and sighed, feeling almost relieved. There were no bodies that he could see.

The cell phone sang its piercing trill from within his pocket and Douglas pulled it out and snapped it open.

"Nicely done, detective," Blythe praised. "Although the use of the radio was cheating. I'm done with the rest of the force. This is our little game, Dougie. No more uninvited players."

"Fuck you," Douglas laughed, delirious with success. "You can go straight to hell with your fucking rules and your little games. I will do whatever it takes to bring you down, Blythe."

"May 18th," Blythe responded.

Douglas swallowed hard and dipped his head. "What did you say?"

"The date on the back of your wife's necklace," Blythe asked. "What does it mean?"

Douglas felt as though he was going to be sick.

"It's not your anniversary," Blythe continued. "It's not her birthday, or yours. What does it mean?"

"Louise," he said, shuddering out the sound over her name.

"Probably some first kiss or first date crap," Blythe guessed. "Am I right?"

"Where is she?"

"Perfectly safe," Blythe promised, "so long as you play by the rules. I would hate for this game to end prematurely."

"Where is Louise?!?" Douglas' voice exploded over the scene, causing those persons who were closest to him to stop and stare.

Blythe just laughed into the phone.

Douglas' eyes fell closed and he hung his head helplessly. He could picture the necklace as clear as the day he gave it to her. Hanging from the end of a row of gold links was a pendant shaped like a lily flower and inlaid with pearl.

"Easier to snag than I would have thought, really," the bomber mused callously. "Didn't do much to protect her, did you?"

"I will find you," Douglas promised. "Mark my words, you coward. I will find you and I will kill you."

The phone hummed as Blythe groaned. "Enough with the clichés, Dougie. We are more than that, you and I. We are not just regular men, oh no. What we do will touch humanity forever. You are a living, breathing, dangerous history. Together we are making something the world will never forget. Let that seep in," he suggested. "Let that marinate. How's it feel to know that you'll be in textbooks and movies and special editions on the news? It's amazing."

Douglas pulled his hair and growled uncontrollably. The phone went silent, and for those few short moments, the world seemed to come to a slow halt. He could feel himself hardening from the inside out as the world he knew and loved cracked and turned to stone right along with him.

Blythe laughed.

"What next?" Douglas managed, hardly keeping the desperation from his voice. "What do I have to do next?"

"First on the list is that you need to ditch the radio," Blythe said in a happy tone.

Douglas took out the radio he had taken from the police officer at the peak and set it on the hood of a nearby police cruiser.

"Excellent," Blythe praised. "This is our game and our game

alone. You should know that it would make me jealous to have other people insert themselves into our moment—"

"—What next?" Douglas demanded, interrupting the end of Blythe's thought. He forced himself to breathe, pushing and sucking air with a progressive hatred.

"There are six more bombs in the city," Blythe informed him.

The weight of doing this six more times hit Douglas square in the lungs. He strained to keep air moving through him.

"Three unwilling helpers are currently sitting on the beach at Junk Bay, just east of Lei Yue Mun," Blythe explained. "Together they have duffle bags with enough C4 to topple a building or at least create a massive hole in the earth."

Douglas pinched his eyes and pictured the scene. There was nothing on that beach but rocks and the scattered tourist or wanderer. The casualties of such a blast would be minimal.

"Three others are sitting at the edge of Hollywood Park," Blythe continued in the same confident voice. "They have just as much C4 stowed in their bags, and I am willing to wager they bring the Central Park Hotel crashing down."

Douglas' mind spun an insane circle.

"You may choose one group," Blythe instructed, his tone growing oddly serious. "Three people will explode today. They are either sitting at the beach or perched in a crammed downtown district. Your choice, but before you go racing off to save one or the other," Blythe added, the satisfaction in his tone rising once again. "There is something I should tell you first. The three people in the park? You don't know them. They're just a few random persons I snatched while coming back from the market."

Douglas shut his eyes tightly and tried not to lose his head.

"The three at the beach, I'm afraid," the bomber continued in a mock sad tone. "Well... You know them quite well."

"Louise," Douglas said, the word escaping from him in a short burst.

"No," Blythe laughed into the phone. "No. I've got something very special planned for her if you don't go dying on me first."

Guilty relief washed over Douglas' trembling face.

"There is Bao, the recorder from the station," Blythe stated first.

Douglas could picture her, young and lively and beautiful. She was a light in the office, and Douglas had a fondness for her that was almost adulterous. His concern burned with a guilty severity.

"And Nuan," the voice over the cell continued.

"You bastard," Douglas cursed, picturing Louise's cousin and closest living relative.

"She put up the biggest fight," Blythe confessed. "And then there is Yun."

Douglas' mind raced back to his home and the little neighbour-hood boy. "The kid?" he asked in a voice of disbelief.

"He fought almost as much as Nuan," Blythe informed the detective. "But Bao? Hell," he chuckled. "She didn't put up a fight at all. Pretty little thing all but went willingly."

Douglas balled his fist and twisted his face into a knot.

"You had forty minutes last time," Blythe said in a calm voice. "These bombs are set to detonate at quarter-till, so you have about thirty-five minutes. That is, of course, as long as the bait does as they were told. If they try to talk to anyone or open their bags, then I hit the button and they go up like fireworks. Who do you think will crack first? The boy? Bao? One of the faceless innocents? They are the hardest to tell, you know. You think they'll just act like good hostages but someone always seems to mess up a plan by doing something stupid."

"You're a monster," Douglas professed.

"I thought I said no more clichés, hmm?" Blythe replied.

Douglas took a breath and looked carefully around him.

"I know you can do it, Detective," the voice on the phone encouraged him. "You can save your friends, or save thousands of faceless bystanders. It's your call."

"This ends today," Douglas promised.

Blythe laughed darkly into the phone. "I'm planning on it."

Blythe set the receiver down on the rotary phone and leaned back in his chair. The apartment would have been completely dark if it wasn't for the glow of the monitors stacked four high and six wide on the desk before him. Each little screen showed a black and white image from a CCTV feed, and the locations were all over the city. There was the pavilion at the peak and Blythe's front yard. There was a school and a dozen shots of crowded intersections.

Off to one side of the monitor, bank was the image of three persons sitting back to back in Hollywood Park, a large black duffle bag draped over each lap. They looked around nervously but said nothing. On the screen below theirs was another trio occupying a rock at Junk Bay. The shot was from behind them, but it was still clear that there was something large and black strapped over their laps.

In the centre of the monitor bank was an image of Douglas, snapping his phone shut and jamming it angrily into his pocket. Blythe watched as the detective spun a slow circle and surveyed the area, snatched a jacket and a hat out of a cruiser, both with the word 'POLICE' in large white letters written across them, then marched off and away from the wreckage. Douglas rounded a corner and disappeared behind a retaining wall.

Blythe tipped back in his chair and lifted his face to the ceiling. It was all going so perfectly.

Douglas moved quickly along the wall and flagged down a passing taxi. The driver pointed to his unlit sign and drove right by with an apologetic shrug. The detective blurted out his irritation then stepped into the road, holding his badge above his head. Several vehicles swerved to miss him, but the street was soon filled with stopped cars. Douglas marched to a taxi and pulled the rear passenger door open. In the back of the cab, a man in a suit recoiled at the aggressiveness shown by the detective and slipped against the far door.

"Police," Douglas announced. "I need this cab."

The man argued and threw his hands up in disgust.

Douglas simply slipped into the seat beside the man and said, "Suit yourself." He then leaned in and whispered, "I'm on my way to disarm a bomb, and you probably do not want to be anywhere near where I'm going."

The businessman leaned back, scowling at Douglas until the realization of the statement hit home. He then pulled the door open and quickly slipped out of the car.

"What did you say?" the cab driver asked in a worried tone.

"Nothing," Douglas replied. "Take me downtown."

Blythe hummed as he drifted through the darkened apartment, sipping on a cup of tea and dancing his fingers to the music from the low radio. He moved to a window and peered through a thick curtain. All around him were tall buildings, bright and shining in the morning sun. The streets below were like those of any major metropolitan city across the globe, full of cars and busy pedestrians, and Blythe looked down upon them with an indifferent pleasure. To him, the world was nothing more than a quietly grinding machine and people were just another cog in the line. Break one, and you can always just replace it with another.

There was an innumerable supply of cogs in the world, and so very few machinists.

Blythe took a deep breath, drawing in the smell of his tea, and sighed loudly at the window. In his mind, he was the answer to the world's lack of ambition. Too many persons lived one day to the next and really did nothing at all. They spun in place, a dead piece in a process they didn't choose. They needed a man like him to come in and bring them back to life.

He was a doctor.

He was a life-saver.

Blythe could bring a man up from his place and make him alive. Men like Detective Inspector Brown.

Moving back to his seat before the monitors, Blythe scanned the screens for any sign of Douglas. He had cameras all over the city and, thanks to his ex-military expertise, could patch into dozens of security feeds at will, but coverage on the streets was still limited.

"No bother," Blythe consoled himself quietly. "The good detective will make the only choice he can."

Several minutes passed with Blythe silently eyeing the monitors. The timer reached the ten-minute countdown and a smile moved over his face.

Blowing up one site would be great, Blythe decided silently, *but if the detective didn't make either, how much more complete would his transformation be if he failed entirely?*

"A new man entirely," he promised aloud. "A brand new man."

Blythe's hopes took a small dip when a taxi screeched to a halt along Hollywood Park. He watched as Douglas got out, still wrapped in his police hat and cap, and felt a twinge of pride.

"You kill your friends," he said in a tone that lacked accusation, "and choose to do the greatest amount of good. When will you see?" he pled, gesturing at the screen. "When will you see that the amount of complacency in the world is so engorged that there is no amount of good that you can accomplish to balance it out. There is no lesser of two evils," he continued, tapping the monitor. "There is simply you, and how your choices affect your existence. Sometimes you need to accomplish something to become a better person, but sometimes," he warned the image on the screen, "pain is the only tool for growth."

Blythe studied the detective as he searched the sidewalks, paths, and benches for any sign of the three package-holders. Douglas moved up and down quickly, keeping his head low and clearly attempting to prevent a stampede. Blythe knew the detective wouldn't just storm in and scream bomb until everyone left, but he was impressed by the way Douglas kept a low-profile and a quick pace.

Finally, the detective found the right bench. Blythe was giddy as he watched Douglas try to talk to the three holding the bombs. They had been instructed to be silent with the threat of detonation, and the detective was having trouble getting them to cooperate. Douglas' gestures were slow and soothing as he slipped one bag off of a lap.

Then the second.

Then the third.

The players in Blythe's game skittered away, and Douglas carefully opened a bag. Blythe wished he could make out the look on the detective's face when he saw all that C4. Instead, he had to settle for being there for the moment when the other bomb detonated, and Douglas would realize that all of his efforts meant nothing when his friends and family were killed.

"Ah well," Blythe said as Douglas finished disconnecting the detonator. "That's life." He turned his attention to the image of the beach and dropped his teacup, which smashed on the tiled floor.

Douglas was on that screen too.

There he was, in the same police coat and hat, pulling bags off of laps and sending the hostages away running.

"No," Blythe breathed.

His eyes darted from screen to screen, checking the times and measuring the images.

"This isn't—" he began, then paused. "Bastard."

The front door suddenly exploded in a blast of splintered parts, falling in on the floor in a crashing spray. Blythe didn't even bother to turn around.

"Hello, detective," he said in a dry tone.

"Hands up, Blythe," Douglas ordered.

The bomber raised his hands to his shoulders and slowly spun in the chair. "Clever," he praised. "Using other officers to stand in your place. I was wondering how you would manage two places at once, but I did not expect you to be in three."

"Life is full of surprises," Douglas reminded him. The detective held his sidearm levelled at Blythe and kept a serious face.

"Isn't it though?" Blythe asked darkly. "So how did you manage it?"

"I've had a tracer on your calls since this morning," Douglas admitted. "I knew you were watching me, but even you couldn't have a camera everywhere. As soon as I was sure I was alone, I contacted the station."

"And yet you are here alone?" Blythe guessed.

"Don't worry," Douglas answered. "The troops will be here soon."

"Not soon enough, I'm afraid," Blythe sighed. The man reached for the sleeve of his jacket and slowly pulled it up his still-elevated arm. A thick watchband was strapped around his wrist, and a small blue light flickered delicately. "It's my heart," he explained, "but it is also your wife's."

"Where is Louise?" Douglas growled, steadying the hold on his pistol.

"Oh, I was hoping it wouldn't really come to this," Blythe admitted. "I wanted to see you blossom, but instead I fear you are beyond recovery."

"Where is Louise?!?" Doug screamed.

"She's on the roof," Blythe confessed, pointing to the monitors.

The topmost screen on the left showed Louise, strapped to a chair with a device taped over her chest.

"So here's the final choice, detective," Blythe announced. "This band is the transmitter and it is set to explode if my heart stops beating." He lowered his hands and adjusted the cuffs of his jacket. "Kill me, and she explodes. Save her, and I will disappear back into the world. You will never get this chance again."

"And how about I just arrest you?" Douglas offered. "What makes you sure that I will kill you?"

"First," Blythe smiled, "because you want to. You may not feel like a killer, but that doesn't change the vengeance in your heart. Second—" Blythe reached into his back waistband and produced a pistol. The gun hung menacingly at the end of his relaxed arm "—I will kill myself if you won't."

"What?"

Blythe raised the gun and pressed the barrel to his head. "I am more alive than you will ever be."

"You are insane," Douglas corrected.

"Three..."

Douglas twisted his face and debated his options.

"Two..."

"Wait," he said.

"One," Blythe said in a resolved tone.

"No!" Douglas said, raising his hands. The detective tossed his gun into a chair across the room and kept his hands up. "I choose Louise."

"Very well," Blythe said, lowering the pistol to his side.

Douglas backed toward the doorway and then disappeared into the hall.

"Too bad," Blythe said, stuffing the gun into his belt. "So much promise." He then flipped a switch on the monitor panel and stepped backed while the table filled with smoke. The monitors sizzled and burned from within until they popped and shot sparks over one another. Blythe watched until he was sure they were all destroyed, then grabbed a duffle bag sitting ready by the door and stepped into the hall. A brick came into view as it slammed into his face. He fell back and landed unconscious on the floor.

"Heart still beating, right?" Douglas asked, tossing the brick to the floor. He took Blythe's gun, handcuffed him, then retrieved his own weapon from the chair. "Now let's go say hi to Louise."

The hallway filled with the sounds of treading boots and muted commands. Police officers poured into the room, weapons ready and their faces hard and focused. Two patrolmen moved through the room to secure the space while three more stood by over Blythe.

"There is a hostage on the roof who may be fitted with an explosive device," Douglas announced, pocketing his radio. He pointed to the pair of patrolmen now returning from their sweep. "You two," Douglas ordered, "watch over the suspect. This is the man we have been hunting. This is the one, and he is more dangerous than either of you can imagine. He doesn't move. You get me?"

The officers nodded.

"You three," Douglas continued, eyeing the other officers. "Come with me."

While the two stayed to watch over Blythe, Douglas and the others raced back to the stairs for the short climb to the roof. When they emerged in the sunlight, the detective choked at the sight. Louise looked to her husband with a broken and terrified expression, tied and gagged in a chair. She was fitted with a black vest that was covered with plastic explosive, and Douglas knew that one false move and the blast would bring down the entire building.

He ran to her and examined the bomb, shushing away her fears. The sight of her face, pink and trembling, and the dry streaks of makeup mixed with fresh tears told Douglas that she had been bound and terrified for some time.

"It's okay," he said, looking over the device and second-guessing himself. The detonator was unlike anything he had ever seen, and he wasn't confident he could disarm it. Louise began to whine from behind her gag, but Douglas did not dare look her in the eye. There was no way he could show his face and still hide his fears.

"Do we have an eight hundred unit en route?" Douglas asked in a calm voice.

The officers shuffled silently and no one answered.

A sick feeling filled Douglas' chest.

"One is at Hollywood Park," an officer finally reported. "And the second—"

"—Is at Junk Bay," the detective finished. Before this moment, Douglas could not have imagined the department needing more than two bomb disposal technicians.

The officer added in a low voice, "The Hollywood team can be here in—"

Douglas put a hand in the air and shook his head. The moments throbbed painfully by as he tried to find the answer. Blythe was out, and he wouldn't help anyway. There was no time to wait for an eight hundred unit to get over here and dismantle the device.

"There has to be a countdown timer," Douglas muttered. He looked over the vest and found a receiver. He knew he could pop it open and then he just had to cut the right wire. But if he cut the wrong one he and every other person in the building would die.

"Order an evacuation," he said in as calm a voice as he could manage.

"Sir?" one of the officers asked.

"Clear the building." The detective wiped his mouth with a shaking hand. "Quick and dirty. Just get as many as possible out as you can."

The officers looked down at Douglas, kneeling before the hostage tied and weighed down with plastic explosives. "Let's go," one of them decided and they jumped into action. As soon as they made the door, Douglas took away the gag from his wife.

"What are you doing?" she demanded.

The sounds of officers ordering people to leave the building rose from the stairwell.

"Sit still," Douglas ordered. "They wouldn't have left me here if they knew you're my wife. They're going to clear the building, and we are going to get you out of this."

"Can you disarm it?"

"No," Douglas admitted in a short and flat tone.

Louise shivered as the realization hit her. "So this is going to go off?"

"I hope not," Douglas replied, untying her from the chair.

"You should leave," she said, her voice grinding and emotional. "I mean it, Doug," she said with more force. "If it goes off, you can't be anywhere near here."

"Louise," Douglas said calmly, still cut\ love you. Now shut up. We're getting you out o. .

"How?" she barked, fresh tears staining her chee. . Can you turn the bomb off?"

"No," he said in a distracted tone. "I'm going to remove the vest."

"What?" Louise snapped.

Douglas took his pocket knife in a trembling hand and looked his wife in the face. "There's C4 wrapped all around you," he tried to explain calmly. "It won't slip over your head, but if I cut the shoulder straps of the vest I bet it will slip down. You've never had much in the way of hips. I'm betting you can step right out of it."

"You're betting?" she asked, panic welling up. "That's your best plan?"

"Yep," he replied while looking under the vest for wires he would want to avoid. "There's nothing over your shoulders but the vest," he said, confidence rising by the moment. "Now don't move."

Carefully and slowly, Douglas nicked away and sliced the shoulders of the vest until the straps laid limply to the front and back.

"Now stand up," Douglas said quietly, "nice and slowly."

He took Louise in one hand and held the vest gingerly in the other. She rose, shaking and sweating until she was standing fully erect. Douglas gave the vest a little twist and it dropped a few inches.

"This is going to work," he announced for both their benefit.

He gave another little twist and the vest settled until the C4 bricks wrapped around Louise like a belt.

"Moment of truth," Douglas said quietly.

Louise chose not to reply. Instead, she placed her hands on her head and closed her eyes. Douglas gave the vest a twist and it wedged tightly over her hip bone. Louise muffled a whimper, and Douglas gave the vest another twist. They could hear the strain of the material as it stretched over her jeans, but Douglas knew it was this or nothing.

"Don't move," he said, and then, without another warning, Douglas pulled the vest in earnest and it popped loudly as it broke loose over her hips and settled on her feet. The pair of them huffed loudly and stared at the other, amazed to still be alive. Douglas lifted one of Louise's feet out, then the other. She took a step and then collapsed to her knees. Douglas jumped up, took the vest in his hand, and ran to the edge of the building.

"What are you doing?" Louise asked. "We need to run."

"We can't leave it here," Douglas decided. "The bay is too far away," he added to himself, "and there's nothing I can drop it in." He moved to the next ledge and looked over.

"Just leave it and let's run!" Louise cried.

Douglas smiled over the edge and then looked back to his wife. The smile disappeared when he saw the officer standing in the stairwell doorway. The look on the patrolman's face told him enough. The man walked onto the roof with empty hands and a terrified expression on his face.

"No," Douglas said just before the shot was fired.

The patrolman's head pitched forward and he fell flat, colliding with the roof like a sack of raw meat. Louise covered her scream but Douglas watched the door. Blythe sauntered out, handcuffs dangling from one wrist and a pistol perched in the other hand. His face was bloody and swollen behind a mangled nose, and his eyes glared red and angry.

"I misjudged you," Blythe said in a twisted voice. "But not again. Say goodbye to your wife." He raised the pistol to his temple and smiled, showing the fresh gaps in his grin.

Douglas dropped the bomb over the edge and drew his pistol. Blythe fired and the detective screamed for Louise to get down. Over the edge, the vest tumbled and snapped in the air until it splashed in the apartment complex's courtyard pool. The explosion shook the building and sent water spraying hundreds of feet into the air, and the sound filled the city for a brief and horrifying moment. Beneath them, the building groaned but stood fast. A mist of warm water floated around them as Douglas pushed himself off to his feet. He looked at Blythe, twisted and bloody by the stairs, and then went to Louise. He pulled her up and wrapped his arms around her. They stood under the sun, policemen flooding the streets and the sound of a helicopter rising in the distance. The city below hummed and buzzed with activity, but the two of them only heard the ragged breath of one another.

"It's over. You're alright. It's over," Douglas repeated as much for himself as for Louise. "Let's go home."

Also Available

False Flag by Jay Tinsiano. (Frank Bowen #1)
ISBN: 978-1-9997232-2-4
1991: A plan to destabilise Hong Kong is emerging; the key players are being put into place, the wheels are in motion and innocent people will die.

An international conspiracy thriller, False Flag spans South-east Asia, with twists and turns that leave every character in question.

Pandora Red by Jay Tinsiano. (Frank Bowen #2)
ISBN: 978-1-9997232-3-1
Frank Bowen's mission is to find a GCHQ whistleblower but in doing so unwittingly risks everything, including his own family's safety.

As part of a covert team, assigned to dangerous missions, Bowen believes he knows what he's up against, until a team of Russian mercenaries are thrown into the mix, leaving everyone and everything hanging in the balance.

It's a race against the clock to save all that he holds dear and uncover the dark truths behind his mission.

White Horse by Jay Tinsiano and Jay Newton. (Dark Paradigm #1)
ISBN: 978-1-9997232-1-7
Half a world away in Spain and running from his past, a Los Angeles gangster unwittingly takes a train that's headed straight

into a terrorist attack. He survives only to face an even deadlier threat.

On that same train: a virologist with clues to a deadly epidemic. Did his secrets die with him in the strike?

Raging in the aftermath, a foul-tempered police chief with a daughter caught in the attack thirsts for revenge. But against whom?

An orphan child without a name disappears down a dark, illegal CIA mind-control programme. Now trained in the ways of death, he prepares to do his master's twisted bidding.

This tale of global conspiracy that threatens humanity itself will keep you guessing whether anyone can survive.

Red Horse by Jay Tinsiano and Jay Newton. (Dark Paradigm #2)
 ISBN: 978-1-9997232-4-8
Haleema Sheraz, a cyber hacker for the Iranian government, discovers her father has gone missing. Frustrated at the lack of urgency from the police, she investigates and soon reveals a kidnapping network that spans back to Operation Paperclip in World War II.

Meanwhile, her brothers join an ISIS-inspired uprising that is wreaking havoc inside Iran, and finding her father quickly becomes a mission to save her family.

Soon they will all be thrust into the battle zone and their lives will change irreversibly in this epic story of bitter struggle against the backdrop of total war.

For more information on the full catalogue visit:
www.darkparadigm.co